WARNING

This book contains sexually explicit scenes and adult language. It may be considered offensive to some readers. This book is for sale to adults ONLY.

* * * * * * * * * * * * * * * * * *

Please store your files wisely where they cannot be accessed by underage readers.

ISBN-13: 978-1773500584
ISBN-10: 1773500589

Other books by Shyla Starr:

<u>Tenacious Billionaire BWWM Romance Series</u>

Adalia is too proud to accept help from the billionaire playboy, Trent Dawson. How long can she maintain her resolve? The bank is at her heels to repossess her business. To make matters worse, Adalia finds suspicious evidence of Trent's philandering ways. She must determine whether to trust Trent with the fate of her business and her heart.

<u>Elusive Billionaire Romance Series</u>

Billionaire Hendrick is trying to repair his company's image by putting in some volunteer work, building a school and hospital for the impoverished children in Africa. There, he meets a beautiful African American volunteer, Jocelyn. They hit it off right away but does she belong in his world?

<u>Lonely Billionaire Romance Series</u>

Tricia was hired to care for billionaire John's wife, who is dying. An unlikely romance emerges after his wife, Rebecca, gives John permission to pursue his happiness after she is gone.

<u>Ardent Billionaire Romance Series</u>

Deirdre doesn't know what to make of the gorgeous man that seems to be interested in her. His name is Parker Walters and he seems friendly enough. There is just something off about him. Why is he trying the hide the fact that he is the heir to his father's billion dollar software empire?

Fervent Billionaire BWWM Romance Series

Alexandra had never been with a white man before. She had seen William at the café before but she always kept her distance. It was unfortunate that their first chance meeting happened when she dropped her breakfast and spilled coffee all over his expensive business suit.

Audacious Billionaire BWWM Romance Series

Chante is torn between staying close to a man beyond her league, and fleeing from him to spare herself from a hopeless position. But she finds she is propelled into a place where she needs to confront her doubts and cast her fate aside to follow the dictates of her heart. Damned if she does and miserable is she doesn't, how will Chante face the events that will lead her to a place of pure happiness or to the pits of a broken heart?

Get the latest update on new releases from the author at:

https://shylastarr.com/newsletter/

This book is Part Four of the "Persuasive Billionaire BWWM Romance Series"

1 - Love Invested

Stacey is trying to keep a handle on her life the best that she can. She is on the verge of losing her job and her apartment, while taking care of her sick grandmother. Her life takes an unexpected turn when she meets Charlie, who works for the construction company that is attempting to persuade her to move out of her home.

2 - Love Divested

After discovering that Charlie has a fiancée, Stacey's world has turned upside down. She cannot help but feel as if she is in over her head. Struggling with her job, her bills and her family, will Stacey be able to figure out how she can get her life straightened out?

3 - Love Reinstated

Stacey decides that she has to put Charlie behind her and move on with her life. As Stacey dates Tony and is pulled into his world, she slowly realizes that although she likes him, it might not be enough to brush aside her feelings for Charlie. Leaving everything behind, she lets herself get lost in the money and privacy that Tony brings to her.

4 - Love Confirmed

Stacey can't believe the turn of events in her life. After losing her grandmother and running away to Tony's private island, she was content to stick her head in the sand and forget her past. But a proposal from Charlie changes everything.

5 - Love Divine

Stacey must ensure she relaxes in order to keep her baby safe. But life is never that easy. Her new husband's father is bent on sabotaging their fledgling investment firm. To make things worse, her brother-in-law isn't content with just being in the background. Stacey finds herself wishing she could have the brothers patch things up.

Persuasive Billionaire BWWM Romance Series

Love Confirmed

Book Four

By Shyla Starr

Table of Contents

Chapter One

EVEN THOUGH it was autumn, the rain was pouring down as if it was one of those summer storms back in the city. The road here wasn't even made out of pavement, but some sort of gravel that stuck to the tires of the car and bounced Stacey around. Her nose was pressed against the passenger side window, as if she could make anything out.

"You alright?" Charlie asked next to her as he slowly rounded a corner.

Stacey cleared her throat. "Nervous."

"You'll be fine. It'll be me that Dad will be flipping his shit over, not you."

He sounded confident, which made sense since it was his father after all. Even so, Stacey couldn't shake the sense of foreboding that was hanging over her. The storm only made her anxiety worse.

"I'm sure you're right," she finally replied, glancing over at him.

The sudden movement made her ring flicker up at her in the dim light. Stacey still wasn't used to seeing it. She wasn't used to what it represented either. She was *engaged* to Charlie. It had been two weeks since their engagement, but it still didn't feel as if it had truly sunk in.

The night that he had decorated the greenhouse and proposed felt like a dream. She clung to the memory now to help her with her nerves. Sure, she had only heard horror stories about Charlie's family. But he was here and would have her back. She had nothing to fear.

"Anyway, just let me handle most of the talking. Dad will be grumpy, but he's always grumpy. He's been that way ever since Mom died," Charlie joked.

His mother. She was one person Charlie had spoken about at length the past couple of weeks. Stacey had never asked him about his mother, mostly because she always sensed that he hadn't wanted to talk about her.

When he finally did, he told her how she had gotten very sick and died when Charlie was eight years old. Eric, his brother, could hardly recall her.

"Dad changed when that happened," Charlie said to her. "It was as if she was the only driving force of good in him. He had always been able to juggle the company and family, but after Mom died… there was no family anymore. Just the company. Always the company."

The words stuck in her head now as they turned onto a larger road. Charlie's father was at their *vacation home* although it was so far out of state and in the country that it wasn't what Stacey pictured when she heard the term. They had been driving for two hours since leaving the airport.

"We're almost there," Charlie said as if reading her mind. "Rain slowed us down a lot."

"Didn't know it rained like this out here."

"Probably just because my dad is in the area." At seeing her face, he cleared his throat. "That was a joke. Sorry. I'm making you more nervous, aren't I?"

"Yes, but I get it. Joking to cope." Stacey smiled weakly.

"One way of putting it," he replied grimly.

Through the front window of the car, Stacey saw it. It was as if it appeared out of nowhere, conjured up by Charlie's joke. Through each wipe of the windshield, she could see a magnificent house before them. It looked more like a manor than just a house.

"Wow," Stacey breathed. "This looks like something I'd picture out of an old novel or something."

"It isn't haunted," Charlie replied, and she looked at him. "What? Don't those old books always have ghosts around the manors? Or the moors. Or something."

"Did you sleep through your fancy English literature class back in college?" she quipped.

Charlie laughed. "Well, it still isn't haunted. Dad just isn't one for being subtle in any occasion. He had this place built after Mom died. Wanted it to look as if it could be dropped down in Scotland and fit right in."

"Well, it definitely looks like that."

They drove through the open iron gates. In the front of the house was a fountain that Stacey could just barely make out through the storm. She looked up to try to see the top of the house. It was decorated with what looked to be gargoyles which only added to the creepy vibe of the place.

Charlie drove around the circular gravel driveway and stopped in front of the manor. The heavy oak doors opened up and two men stepped out. The taller man was holding an umbrella. Together, they walked over to them. One of them opened the back doors of the car and began removing luggage. The other came over to the passenger door and opened it.

"Peter!" Charlie exclaimed, leaning over. "How are you?"

"Good, sir. I've brought an umbrella to escort your fiancée to the front door. Then I can come back to fetch you."

"I'll catch up with you," Charlie said to Stacey.

She nodded and clutched her purse, feeling oddly nervous. She stepped out of the car and was staring at Peter. He was an older-looking man. His hair had gone completely grey and he was slightly hunched over. She reached for the umbrella, but he shook his head once and then turned around to lead her to the front door.

Stacey hurried after him, not wanting to get wet. At the front doors, he ushered her inside. A quick glance showed that the other man was behind her, holding all their luggage. The rain didn't seem to affect him at all. Even so, she felt badly for him.

The door closed behind her and Stacey looked around. They were in what seemed to be an entrance hallway. There was nothing modern about this place. Everything looked old-fashioned as if from an old horror movie set. The hallway was narrow, and the floors were made of hard wood. There was a staircase next to her. Not even one of those spiraling staircases she had been seeing so often lately but a cramped one that reminded her a little of the one on Tony's yacht.

The walls were decorated with paintings, mostly landscapes. The place smelled faintly of mothballs. This was not what Stacey had been expecting. This looked like a place someone who came from old money would live in, not a place that someone would intentionally build.

The front door opened again and Charlie came in. He was soaking wet and holding some of the luggage.

"Sir, I was going to come back for you," Peter said.

"I'm fine, thanks. I didn't want to leave Warren with all the luggage," Charlie replied.

Warren, who looked even older than Peter, smiled a toothy grin. "I'll dry these off and bring them to your rooms."

"Thanks. Wait, uh, rooms?" Charlie asked.

Warren's eyes flicked over to Peter, who spoke up, "Yes, sir. Master Terrence has requested you two sleep in separate rooms since you are not married. It would be improper."

I really have stumbled into some sort of time machine, haven't I? Stacey thought glumly. She looked over at Charlie to see if he was going to say anything. He had said before arriving here that he was going to have to pick his battles, especially with his news. Separate rooms would be weird, but it didn't seem like something to kick a fuss over.

Charlie's lips pressed together in a thin line but he nodded his head in agreement. Stacey relaxed a little. Better not to start things off with a fight about bedrooms. Peter moved past Stacey and began to walk up the stairs.

"This way, please," he said to the two of them without looking back.

Stacey shot Charlie a look but all he did was wiggle his eyebrows in an attempt to make her laugh. They walked up the staircase. The first floor had the same décor as the one below. Paintings along the walls. A carpet that was full of dull colors. The windows were opened, showing the pouring rain outside. All the doors were closed. They stopped at one near the end of the hallway.

"This is your room, sir," Peter said to Charlie, opening it for him.

Stacey peered inside. It was a large room with its own bathroom. The bed was huge and could have easily fit the two of them. There was a couch and a bookshelf on the other wall with a table in front of it.

"Warren will bring your bags up once they're cleaned off, sir."

"Great, thanks. Stacey is going to be next to me?" Charlie asked.

"No, sir. Master Terrence has put Stacey on the fifth floor."

"The fifth floor?" Charlie and Stacey exclaimed in unison.

Peter's face didn't change. All he did was nod. She glanced over at Charlie who looked as if he was about to open his mouth and tell Peter off. Stacey rested her hand on his arm.

"It's fine. It's just a big house, right? Not the end of the world to be on the fifth floor."

"The fifth floor is reserved for guests, ma'am, while these rooms are for family. Nothing personal," Peter said to her.

"Of course. Not a problem. I'll see you later." She directed this to Charlie who still looked furious but nodded in reply.

Stacey followed Peter down the hallway. It wasn't that she liked being shoved up to the fifth floor. It was more that she knew Charlie's announcement of leaving the company was going to go off like an atom bomb. She didn't want him to lose his patience early over small things like this.

They went up the flights of stairs to Stacey's guest room. When they stepped into this hallway, Stacey found it hard to believe that it was just for guests. Since it was closest to the roof, it was more cramped than the other hallways. Some of the doors here were open, showing off small rooms filled with mostly clutter. At the end of the hallway was a window that overlooked the gardens. A closet was next to it filled with supplies.

It was the door next to the supply closet that Peter unlocked. The fact it could be locked from the outside was alarming. He opened the door.

"Here you are, ma'am. Master Terrence will see you at dinner. Thank you."

Before she could ask anything, he turned and walked down the hallway. Stacey watched him go and then looked at her own room.

It was a pale comparison to Charlie's room. The room was slanted due to the roof and was cramped. There was a twin bed shoved against the wall and a dresser in the other corner. A rug had been tossed down onto the floor. That was it. Stacey wasn't even sure where the bathroom was on this floor.

She went over and gingerly sat at the edge of the bed which squeaked. It was obvious what Charlie's father meant by this. Putting her up on the fifth floor meant she didn't matter. Putting her in what was basically a broom closet said that he had already made up his mind about her.

"Great," she mumbled to herself.

Chapter Two

The rain didn't stop. Her own small window gave her the view of basically the driveway, but Stacey couldn't make out anything. She wondered if she could go find Charlie. But the fear of pissing off his father made her stay in place. It was probably a good idea that Charlie come to fetch her rather than run the risk of her being caught creeping around the manor.

She wasn't sure what she was waiting for and was busy trying to quell her nerves when there was a knock on the door. Stacey rushed over, hoping it was Charlie, and opened the door.

"Hi, ma'am. Brought the luggage by."

It wasn't Warren who stood before her but someone new. Stacey wondered just how many people worked in this house to keep it running. The situation seemed silly when basically it was only Terry and Charlie's brother, Eric who apparently lived here.

The man in front of her was dressed plainly and smelled of cigarette smoke. Had he snuck off before bringing her the luggage? Stacey felt a little prick of relief. Someone working here who was a bit normal and had a secret. That was something, at least.

"Hi, uh, thanks. Thanks for bringing them up." She went to grab them as she said, "I can put them in here."

"I got it," the man said to her, brushing by her with her luggage.

He put her things down on the floor and looked around. "Man. He sure shoved you into a shit hole, didn't he?"

Stacey blinked. "Excuse me?"

"Master Terrence. This place looks like it used to be a supply closet or something. Probably was. We shove a bunch of stuff on the fifth floor." He turned to look at her. "Not that you're 'just a bunch of stuff', ma'am."

She was surprised by his candor. Peter and Warren had both seemed to be on auto-pilot. They had probably worked here for ages. The man looked around the room as if he was thinking of something. He had a receding hairline and looked older, as if he had been through a lot before settling down here.

"Ah, well." She struggled for something to say. "It's fine."

"Really? Isn't Master Charles on the first floor? Seems a bit unfair but…" He shrugged at her.

"No, it's just – I don't want to rock the boat, you know? Anyway, it's just a room. Besides, this place is really nice."

The man wrinkled his nose. "Yeah, it's alright, I suppose."

"Have you worked here long?" Stacey asked curiously.

"Way too long." He grinned at her and it changed his entire face. He didn't look as run into the ground when he was smiling, Stacey thought.

"Do you happen to know where the bathroom is?"

"Yeah, I'll show you." He motioned for her to leave the room first.

Stacey felt silly at needing someone to show her where the bathroom was, but she followed him anyway. It was located at the very end of the hallway and was just as small as the rest of the rooms. She peered inside.

"Thanks so much."

"No problem. Sorry it's like a dollhouse up here."

"It's completely fine, trust me. From where I came from, even these small rooms are nice." She turned to look at him. "I didn't get your name."

"Devin."

"Nice to meet you. I'm Stacey." She held out her hand.

Devin smiled at her, a slow smile that seemed to spread out across his face as he shook her hand. "Nice to meet you too."

"Well, I should probably freshen up before dinner. Do I just... sorta stick around or what?"

"Someone will let you know when it's ready." He leaned forward and lowered his voice, "Listen, Terry and Eric are assholes. Between you and me."

"Yeah, I haven't exactly heard kind things," she whispered back.

Devin's eyes flicked up to hers. "From Charlie?"

"Yeah. Anyway, I'm sure it'll be okay. I'll just keep my head down. Try not to attract any attention. Are they the only two here?"

Devin clicked his tongue against the roof of his mouth, "Yup. Well, listen, you do that. Don't attract attention. Just let Terry and Eric deal with Charlie. Terry, you know, he'll be furious over the fact you aren't Adele, but he's always pissed off nowadays. Probably because he's dying and all."

Once again, Stacey was surprised at how open Devin was. Secretly, she was glad for the advice. It felt as if someone here was at least on her side. Still, she wasn't sure what to say about Terry being ill from his stroke.

Devin seemed to sense this. He leaned forward even more. They were quite close now and it made her feel a little uncomfortable. She could smell mint on his breath, as if he had tried to cover up the cigarette smell.

"See you later."

She nodded and watched as he turned to go. Devin looked back once and smiled at her. Then he was down the stairs without another word. Stacey shut the bathroom door behind her. Stay low. Don't attract attention. It was advice she was going to listen to as much as she could.

<<◇>>

When Charlie appeared at her door an hour later, she swung her arms around him and crushed him in a hug.

"Whoa, everything okay? You didn't see a ghost, did you?" Then he gently pushed her away and stepped into the room. "What the fuck is this?"

"My room."

"This is not a room," he said, pointing to the floor. "This was a fucking supply closet or something before." He kicked the rug out of its position. "Look. You can see marks from where they dragged stuff out of here."

He was right. Even from here, Stacey could see deep marks in the wood from where something had been dragged away. She shrugged.

"It's fine. I was told that anyway."

But Charlie wasn't listening. "This is so like him. So like my father to pull this shit. God, you know what? I was nervous before about telling him I was leaving the company. But why? We won't have to tolerate stuff like this once we get married and I'm working on my new business. Dad can put Eric in charge or take control again on his own. It won't matter."

"Whoa, whoa, calm down," Stacey said, coming over to him. "Don't get worked up before we go downstairs."

Charlie ran his hand through his hair, looking frustrated. "I know. Dad does things like this just to throw me off. Listen, he's going to be an asshole. So will Eric. But, just let me handle it, alright? Ignore whatever they throw your way. Eric is a moron to begin with."

"When are you going to tell them about the business?" Stacey asked.

"I don't know. When the time is right. Dad thinks this is just for him to meet you since I told him we were engaged."

Stacey thought about what Devin had said and replied, "He isn't going to like me very much. I'm not Adele."

"Thank God for that. Come on. I don't want to be late."

He looped his arm around hers and together they headed downstairs. Stacey tried not to feel nervous, but it was proving difficult.

"No elevator before you ask," Charlie said to her as they looped down to the third floor.

"Any reason why?"

"Didn't fit in with the manor."

As they made it back down to the first floor, Charlie stopped for a moment. Stacey paused and looked down the stairs. The entrance was empty. She was trying to collect herself. This was just Charlie's father. A human being. She had to stop making it worse than it really was. How much had she gone through to be with Charlie? They were engaged now. She wasn't going to let some old man run her off.

"Wait," Charlie said to her. "Who told you that room was a supply closet?"

"One of the people working here. What do you call them? I'm not calling them servants. That feels so old-fashioned. Butler or something?"

"Which one? Warren? Because Peter would have never told you that," Charlie said urgently.

As if he had heard his name, Peter was suddenly at the base of the stairs. "Sir and ma'am, dinner is about to be served. If you could please come this way." He bowed his head.

Charlie gripped her hand tightly. Whatever he was going to ask died on his lips when Peter appeared. Stacey had no choice but to follow him, wondering why he seemed so bothered. They walked down the steps and headed down the hallway.

They were in the living room now. A fire was roaring in the fireplace. Books lined the shelves. There was no TV here. The floor was covered in a thick carpet and the windows had the curtains drawn. It was hot in here and Stacey hoped it wasn't going to feel like this in the dining room.

She lowered her voice as they walked through, "This place is…"

"Creepy? Weird? Mom would have fucking hated it," Charlie whispered back grimly.

They were led down another short hallway before entering the dining room. Here there were more windows. The curtains weren't drawn, allowing Stacey to see the lit patio. It was still raining, so all she could see were puddles and darkness just outside the light. The table in the center looked to be one solid piece of oak. There were places set for everyone. Stacey noticed one of the places was separate from the rest.

"No," Charlie said simply and crossed the marble flooring to move the place setting with the rest.

"Sir –" Peter began to say but Charlie raised his hand to cut him off.

Then he motioned for Stacey to come over. He pulled out the chair and she sat down. He sat down next to her. No one else was there. Peter came over and served them wine. Neither of them moved to take a sip.

Peter left and they sat there in silence for a full minute.

"Are we early?" Stacey finally asked.

Charlie slid out his phone from his pocket and began checking his e-mails. "No. Just my father being his typical self."

"You get service here?"

"Don't be fooled. This place has wi-fi and one of the rooms on the first floor is completely modern; TV, video game systems, state of the art computer. Eric threw a fit when he was younger." He looked away from his phone. "Which reminds me –"

"My older brother!" A voice rang out, breaking the silence and ending Charlie's question.

Charlie stood up and Stacey followed. It felt sort of silly, standing up like that when someone entered the room. But she realized shortly after it wasn't because Eric was coming in. It looked more as if Charlie was trying to get to Eric first. He walked past Stacey toward the dining room entrance.

Eric came into view and Stacey's eyes widened in surprise. He was wearing a tuxedo, while Charlie was just wearing a suit. Yet it wasn't the tux that was taking her back.

It was the fact that Eric was Devin.

Chapter Three

Eric's gaze landed on Stacey and a lazy grin bloomed across his face. Stacey felt her mouth go dry. She was sure that she was blushing. Stupid, stupid. Charlie had his hand gripping Eric's arm. She could practically see the lecture falling out of his mouth. He had figured it out. That was why he had been trying to ask her about it.

Stacey was wondering if he was wearing the tuxedo as more of a joke than anything else. He didn't seem to be listening to Charlie at all. From this view, she couldn't understand how Eric was the younger sibling. There didn't seem to be anything of Charlie in him. He looked almost ten years older than his brother.

"Man, are you done yet?" Eric finally spoke up. "We should all be sitting down when Dad gets here or he's gonna flip."

He broke free of Charlie's grip and sauntered over to the table. Stacey still felt embarrassed. She had honestly fallen for his trick. She had even told him that Charlie had called him basically an asshole. Great.

He stopped in front of Stacey. He was still smiling. Now that she knew he was Charlie's brother, she tried to see any similarities between the two. Yet there was nothing.

"Nice to meet you," Eric said to her through his grin.

Part of her wanted to smack him. The other part of her knew he would probably like it. So she exhaled slowly and forced her own smile on her face.

"We met earlier. Is your memory alright?"

Something flickered behind Eric's gaze. It was unreadable.

"We did, didn't we?" he laughed. "How is the supply closet?"

"Lovely. How is it living up to your reputation as an asshole?" It rolled off her tongue before she could stop herself.

Behind her, Charlie snorted in both laughter and surprise. Eric didn't lose the grin on his face. It was as if her insult hadn't affected him at all. He just chuckled and walked past her. He pulled out the chair across from Charlie and sat down.

Stacey and Charlie sat down as well. She wished she didn't have to be at this dinner. Having Eric successfully trick her made her feel stupid.

Eric pulled out his own phone and began to play a game on it. He had the volume turned up as loud it could go, and it seemed to bounce off the walls. Stacey

leaned over to Charlie and lowered her voice as much
as she could.

"I thought you said that he was younger than you."

"He is."

"He looks a lot older than you."

"It's the receding hairline. Going bald early.
Anyway, he looks like my father. I'm pretty sure my
dad was born looking eighty."

She was going to ask more when two large doors on
the other side of the room opened. Peter walked in first,
helping a man with a cane. Eric didn't stop playing the
game on his phone. But Charlie stood up to go over to
him.

"Want some help?" he asked.

"No! I can sit down by myself," his father barked.

"No problem, Dad," Charlie replied quickly,
hurrying back to his seat.

Terry grunted and slowly made his way toward the
table. For the first time, Stacey could see him clearly.
He was small, as if he had shrunk over the years. The
cane wobbled with each step. She was half worried he
was going to topple over. He sat down at the head of
the table. Peter helped him push in his chair.

"You can go," Terry said to him and he nodded his
head, moving away from the table.

Charlie had been right. Now that she was seeing his father, she could see how Eric looked similar. They both looked older than their age. In Terry's case, he looked positively ancient. Lines were deeply etched in his face and he was balding. His clothes were a size too large for him as if he had lost a lot of weight recently.

Even though he looked feeble, there was a confidence in his movements, as if he didn't care that he was moving slowly or he appeared ill. His eyes had a sort of mischievous look to them – the same sort of look Eric had in his eyes. Yes, Charlie's brother definitely took after their father.

Two more people came out of the kitchen carrying bowls which were served to each person at the table. Stacey looked down to see it was some sort of stew. It smelled delicious, but she didn't want to start eating until Charlie did just in case there was some strange rule in place here.

"Eric, put your fucking phone away. And why the hell are you wearing a tuxedo?" Terry snapped.

Eric made a show of sighing heavily before shoving his phone in his pocket and replied, "Big brother is here. I thought we were all going to dress up. I guess I misjudged his importance." He lingered on the last word.

"We never wear tuxedos to dinner," Terry said. "Don't be stupid."

"That's all he knows how to be," Stacey heard Charlie mumble under his breath.

"Careful, brother. You wouldn't want to rock the boat."

Charlie's face scrunched up as he tried to figure out Eric's meaning. Stacey got it, however. She had said something similar, back when she had thought Eric was Devin. She refused to look at him now and instead became fixated on her spoon in front of her.

"Enough," Terry said and his booming voice caused the two brothers to fall silent. "I'm starving."

He still hadn't said anything to her. Stacey felt almost invisible. In fact, if it hadn't been for Eric's jab at her just now, she could have sworn that she had vanished into thin air. Charlie began to eat. She did as well. The meal was delicious. It had been a long time since Stacey had eaten stew. If only the company were better.

No one spoke. Stacey could hear the rain against the window. Somewhere nearby a clock was ticking. She could probably hear a pin drop at this rate. She glanced at Charlie out of the corner of her eye as if to say *what the hell*? but he didn't look at her.

It was Eric who finally spoke, "So. Stacey. Tell us about yourself."

"Don't," Charlie answered.

"Don't what?" he replied with a cool indifference.

"I know what you're doing."

"Oh, do you?" Eric's tone was mocking now.

"Yes, so why don't you just focus on your dinner instead of starting things?"

Stacey couldn't help but look at Terry. He kept his eyes down on his bowl and ate silently. Eric and Charlie continued to bicker. She suddenly wished she could be anywhere but here.

"You sure have a bad attitude," Eric was saying, "probably because you only hang out with assholes. No offense, Stacey."

The fact that Eric was the only one actively engaging her was weird enough. She knew that Terry would be furious she wasn't Adele but to go so far as to shove her to the fifth floor, move her placement down the table, and now actively ignore her felt like she was dealing with a high school mean girl rather than an old man.

"Charlie," Terry finally spoke up and the two brothers went silent as if someone had unplugged them. "We need to go over the financials while you're here."

"I have people hired to do that."

"Subpar accountants. I want to look at them."

"Dad, that isn't needed. I have it under control –"

Terry held up one of his hands to silence him. His fingers were long and so skinny they looked more skeletal than anything else. Charlie fell silent. Stacey had never seen him act like this before. Bickering with his brother and falling silent when his father ordered it – it was a new side to Charlie, from her point of view.

Everyone went back to eating. Eric finished first. He made a show of dropping his spoon in the bowl. Then he looked at Charlie as if the two were in a race or something. Stacey was full but made herself finish the entire bowl. She was scared of looking rude for not eating all of it.

When Terry finished, he looked up and shouted for Peter. He appeared in the doorway and helped Terry get to his feet.

Charlie stood up and spoke quickly, "Dad, you can't be leaving already?"

"Tired," was all Terry replied.

"But Stacey –" Charlie said, motioning to her.

"Tomorrow we go over the financials. Goodnight."

Charlie stood there, his hands clenching into fists, as Terry was escorted out of the room by Peter. Someone came out of the kitchen and began to clear the dishes. Eric clapped his hands together loudly, which made Stacey flinch.

"Good job."

"What?" Charlie snapped.

"Dad didn't say one word to your fiancée the entire meal. Off to a great start, don't you think?"

"He'll come around."

"Will he? It isn't as if you really put your best foot forward there."

"What the hell does that mean?"

Eric stood up and yawned, as if the entire dinner had bored him to tears. "You're smart. Figure it out. Now, it was a truly wonderful dinner but I'm simply exhausted. Stacey, hope you had a nice time."

He gave her a small wave and left the room. The two of them were alone in the cavernous dining hall. She looked at Charlie. In this lighting, he looked exhausted. Even when he had spent long nights at the office he didn't look this tired. Feeling sorry for him, she reached out and took his hand in hers.

"Sorry," he said to her.

"For what?"

"I had this big plan in my head for how that dinner should go. I was going to introduce you and run through all sorts of conversations. But as soon as I saw Dad, it was as if all of that just flew away. Instead, I acted like the same pathetic little kid like I always do."

"Hey, it's okay. I mean, your dad is sorta scary for an old guy. He just doesn't even look nice," Stacey said, shaking his hand a little to try to make him smile.

Charlie did smile but it looked forced. "Everything he does, he does as some sort of passive-aggressive insult. It's all his childish way of saying he doesn't accept you. I should have stuck up for you. I'm sorry."

"It's only the first night. Don't be so hard on yourself."

"I just don't want to make things bad before I drop the bomb on him about me leaving," he said, lowering his voice.

"I get it. Come on. Let's get out of this room. It's cold and uninviting," Stacey remarked, pulling him toward the hallway.

"That's the entire house," he quipped.

Chapter Four

"How did you know it was Eric?" Stacey asked as they made their way toward the first floor.

"What?"

"When I mentioned that someone had told me the room was a supply closet. You knew."

"Dad has Peter and Warren to help out around the house and a couple of different people to help out in the kitchen. None of them would have told you that it used to be a supply closet. Eric is the only person here who would pull something like that."

"I fell for it too. I should have known."

"Don't blame yourself. You had no idea it was him. He doesn't look like my brother at all. And unfortunately, he is." They stopped in front of his bedroom door.

Stacey wanted to ask more – about his family and the house – but Charlie wrapped his arms around her waist and pulled her in for a kiss. It felt like ages since she had touched his lips. In reality, it hadn't been that long. But every second without him touching her felt like decades.

He pulled her into the bedroom, closing the door behind him. His lips were on her neck so softly that she could barely feel them, yet it was just enough to send goosebumps along her skin.

Their lips met again. This time the kiss was deeper. Charlie's tongue met her own and he made a tiny gasp of pleasure, pressing himself against her. She was against the wall now. His hands were trailing along her arms, pinning them above her head as he kissed her harder.

Stacey liked feeling him flattened against her like this. She liked the thrill of being pinned against the wall. She could feel her heart hammering in her chest as his fingers laced through hers.

Charlie moved down to her neck again, biting it gently before switching to kisses. Stacey closed her eyes, marveling at how each touch seemed to bring her alive. She should be used to it by now, surely. Didn't people say it wore off after time? Yet with Charlie, each time felt like the first time he had touched her.

His hands slid off hers, moving down to her waist. Her dress, which she had changed quickly into before dinner, bunched up around her thighs. Stacey could hear his labored breathing against her ear as he shuffled her skirt up.

Their lips crushed together now so hard that she could feel his teeth against her lips. He bit on her bottom lip, tugging on it. Her hands wrapped around his neck, bringing him as close as possible.

Charlie raised her dress up around her hips. The cold air of the room struck her skin. She shivered, and she could feel him smile against her neck. His hands were fumbling with her belt now. Finally, he loosened the buckle allowing the belt to drop onto the floor.

Stacey yanked on his pants, eager to unzip them. She could feel how hard he was against the fabric, straining for release. She unzipped his pants and tried to lower them. Yet his hand gripped her wrist and moved it away.

"So impatient," he teased, his voice sounding hoarse. "Now, you have to be quiet."

Stacey wasn't sure exactly what he meant until he hooked her underwear aside with one finger and ran another finger down the front of her exposed wet pussy. The touch was sudden and caused her to gasp in surprise.

"Shush, shush," Charlie mumbled in her ear which only made her feel light-headed.

He moved his finger down again, teasing her once more. His fingers were warm, contrasting with how cold the room felt. She breathed heavily. With his other free hand, he kept her wrists pinned above her head against the wall. Stacey couldn't move. All she could do was try to wiggle her hips to have Charlie give her more.

Finally, he relented. He moved his index finger inside of her pussy so slowly that Stacey could hardly stand it. She exhaled and swallowed her moan before she made too much noise. Charlie was studying her face. His lips were parted a little from their kissing and his face was flushed. She could still feel his hard cock through his pants, pressing against her leg.

He began to move his finger in and out of her, so slowly that Stacey wanted to snap at him to give her more. But she didn't – it would only encourage Charlie to continue teasing her. After a minute of this, he slid another finger into her. Stacey's eyes fluttered and she breathed hard.

"You have to keep quiet. Do you think you'll be able to do that for me?" he whispered in her ear.

"Yes," she pleaded.

"Ah, too loud. What did I just say?" he replied, shoving his fingers all the way inside of her.

The sudden motion caused her to gasp. Charlie smiled at her and leaned forward, dragging his lips across her neck. His grip on her wrists was still tight.

"I'll be quiet," she whispered.

Charlie pulled his fingers out from her. Stacey could hardly think straight. All she wanted was to feel him inside of her before she exploded. He kissed her hard, her own lips pressing against her teeth as he took his hand off her wrists and his pants dropped down to his knees. Both of his hands gripped her waist now and he suddenly picked her up.

Stacey wrapped her legs around his waist. Her back was pressed against the wall. Charlie's cock entered her in one swift motion. Going from nothing inside of her to his thick dick made her moan in surprise.

One of his hands covered her mouth swiftly. He began to fuck her like that – Stacey pinned against the wall with his cock deep inside of her and his hand covering her mouth. She whimpered against it, the sound muffled as he thrust deep inside of her.

Charlie himself was quiet. He was breathing heavily but otherwise didn't make a sound. Somehow, that turned her on even more than if he had been moaning. Her hands gripped his back. Her nails dug into the fabric of his shirt. Her dress clung to her, and she could feel sweat on the back of her neck.

Stacey couldn't hold back any longer. She gasped against his hand and closed her eyes. Her climax rolled through like a wave, sending warmth throughout her entire body. Charlie grunted as well. She could feel his cock twitch inside of her as he came. She shuddered against him and buried her face in his neck as they climaxed together.

They clung to each other like this for a full minute. Stacey couldn't even feel her legs. Her entire body felt like jelly. Slowly, Charlie pulled away from her and gently lowered her feet to the floor. Stacey wavered for a moment and pressed her hands against the wall.

"You alright?" he whispered.

"Yeah, just sort of feel like a tire iron hit me. In a good way," she added on quickly.

Charlie laughed shakily and went over to the bed before collapsing on it. He motioned for her, but she shook her head.

"No way. I won't ever get up. I don't want your dad finding us like this," she replied.

It hadn't mattered. Charlie let out a loud snore. He had fallen asleep instantaneously. Stacey marveled at how quickly that had been. She was jealous, actually, mostly because it usually took her ages to fall asleep.

With one last look at him, she crept out of the room.

Stacey quietly closed the bedroom door behind her. Even out here in the hallway, she could hear Charlie snoring. She knew that she could stay in bed with him if she wanted to. But she was still hoping to impress Terry somehow. It would cast a favorable light on her if Terry knew she had respected his wishes. Better to go back to her small bedroom and sleep there.

Yet the silence of the manor seemed to be overwhelming as she stood there in the hallway. She didn't feel tired at all. Stacey walked down the hallway slowly. At one point, she stopped in front of one of the closed doors. She looked around, as if someone were just hanging around spying on her, and then opened it.

It was a guest bedroom. It was ready for someone to use it. Eric and Charlie had been right. Terry had shoved her up on the fifth floor as a dig against her. There were clearly rooms to spare here.

Suddenly feeling awake and slightly rebellious, Stacey went downstairs instead of up. She strolled into the living room. The fire had been put out. There were lamps against the walls which were on the lowest setting. The dimly lit room looked like something she would have dreamt about as a kid. There were strange shadows cast everywhere, and the portraits of people she didn't know looked spookier at night.

Stacey went over to the mantle by the fireplace, drawn to the fact she had thought she had seen framed photos. She stopped in front of it and peered at one of them. It was an old photo of a much younger Terry standing next to a beautiful pale woman. Her hair was chestnut brown and looped up in a simple bun. She was wearing a plain yet striking white dress and holding a bouquet of flowers.

Stacey realized this was most likely Charlie's mother. She picked up the framed photo to get a closer look. Terry was dressed in a tuxedo and was beaming into the camera. There was a thin layer of dust over the photo which she rubbed off to try to see it better.

It was hard to make out the exact features of Charlie's mother, but she could see how they looked similar. Their smiles were almost exactly the same. Their hair color was the same as well. There was also something gentle that Charlie had that his mother had in the photo too.

She put the photo down and looked at the rest of them. They were all older photos. Eric, looking old even as a teenager, dressed up for prom. His arm was slung around a pretty woman and he was grinning into the camera as if he were on top of the world. A photo of Charlie graduating from college. He was standing next to Terry. His posture was stiff. Terry looked grumpy even in this picture. If Stacey hadn't just seen him smiling in his wedding photo, she would have wondered if he was capable of smiling at all.

There was one more photo at the end of the mantle. It caught her eye because the frame was a bright silver and decorated with flowers. Stacey picked it up and stared at it.

It showed Charlie standing next to Adele. Her throat tightened at the sight of them. Adele was dressed in a sleek black suit. She had her arm looped around Charlie's. Her smile looked similar to a great white before it ate its prey. Charlie was looking off to the side as if he was distracted. It was a bad photo. Adele looked as if she had won a prize and Charlie looked as if he were trying to escape.

Even so, Terry had deigned that it was important enough to make it onto the mantle, next to Charlie's graduation portrait and his own wedding photo. It was clear that he had thought they were really going to get married. He'd had his heart set on Adele marrying into the family.

The room felt very musty all of a sudden. Stacey wanted some fresh air. She put the photo down, resisting the urge to place it face down. There were doors leading outside on the other side of the living room and she went to them quickly. Stacey wanted to get away from the cloying scent of mothballs and that photo on the mantle.

It was cold outside. Luckily, the rain had stopped and the sky had cleared. The moon was full in the sky, illuminating the gardens in front of her. It felt as if they went on forever. She could probably wander into them and get lost.

Stacey stepped off the patio and took in a deep breath. The air felt clean compared to the stale air back in the manor. She followed the pathway, letting it take her along the grounds. It was nice to be out of the house. It felt as if she had the entire place to herself.

Just as she was thinking about how nice it was being alone, she saw Eric by one of the fountains. His back was to her. She could see the smoke trail from his cigarette. He hadn't seen her yet. Stacey decided she'd turn around and go the other way.

Yet as she turned, Eric spoke, "I know you're there."

Stacey froze and cursed inwardly. How childish would it be to break out in a run? Knowing Eric, he would probably chase after her just to piss her off. She stayed in place. He turned around and took a long drag off his cigarette.

"Wow, you know, I didn't know anyone even smoked anymore," Stacey remarked.

He exhaled, and the smoke formed a perfect circle. She fought the urge to roll her eyes.

"Didn't expect you to be creeping around. Figured you'd be safe in bed."

"Needed some air. Not like it's any of your business."

"Have a nice dinner?" Eric asked her as he walked over to her.

"The stew was good," she said honestly.

He laughed, "Sure was. Conversation though… not so good."

Stacey shrugged. She didn't know what to say. She felt as if she had babbled enough when she had thought he was part of the house staff. The last thing she was going to do was babble to Eric about how uncomfortable dinner was.

"You know what my favorite part was?" Eric said as he took another drag off his cigarette. "The fact that Charlie didn't mention you at all. I mean, you noticed that, right?"

She had. But the last thing she was going to do was tell Eric that it had bothered her or made her feel uncomfortable.

Eric took her silence as a sign to keep going because he said, "Actually. Now that I'm reflecting on the meal, I think I mentioned you. I did, didn't I? Twice or something."

Stacey fought down her annoyance and turned her head to look at him, "How kind of you."

Eric turned his face away from hers and blew out smoke. Stacey watched it waft up to the sky before it dissipated. In the distance, she could faintly hear thunder.

"Just saying. Kinda shitty of him. You're his fiancée, yet he didn't even bring you up. Guess he's still afraid of Dad."

"Says the guy who sneaks out here for a smoke and then shoves mints in his mouth to try to mask the scent."

Eric actually looked surprised at this. He turned to look at her. His eyes squinted as if she were far away.

A slow smile spread out across his face. "You're not like the other women he's been with. Has he told you that?"

"I don't really care about his old relationships."

"Well. That's half true, right? You care about Adele."

"Why would I care about her?" Stacey asked stiffly.

"Because Dad is so keen on her."

"Why don't you marry her then?"

His cigarette finished, Eric dropped it and crushed the butt under his shoe. Then he pulled out a pack from his pocket. He had changed from his tuxedo into sweatpants and a black t-shirt. He pulled out another smoke and offered the pack to her.

"Want one?"

"No," she paused and added, "thanks though."

Eric slipped the cigarette in between his lips and brought out his lighter. "I don't want to marry Adele. I don't want to get married at all." He flicked the lighter and the flame flickered in the darkness. "No thanks."

Stacey watched the tip of the cigarette glow. She couldn't help but ask, "Why not?"

Eric inhaled deeply before answering, as if he were thinking of a proper way to reply. In spite of her best attempts, she found herself curious to hear his answer.

"Why bother? I don't want to be tied down. Maybe Charlie has to get married because Dad wants him to have a wife and kids to eventually take over the company, but since I'm not in charge, who cares?"

Stacey thought of Charlie's announcement and tried to ask casually, "What if you were?"

"What?"

"What if you were in charge? Would you get married then?"

Eric stared at her for a long moment and she wondered if he was going to figure out that Charlie was leaving.

But instead, he replied with, "Doesn't matter. I'm not in charge. Although… I guess if I was, I'd probably find someone who just wanted to marry me for money."

"What?" Stacey exclaimed, thinking of her sister and Jacob.

"Yeah, why not?" He puffed on his cigarette thoughtfully. "That way, I wouldn't really be tied down. She'd have the money and be happy. I'd have the marriage, so Dad would leave me the hell alone. I'd still have the girlfriends. All works out."

Stacey wrinkled her nose. What was it with these people and marrying just to sort things out for the business? She couldn't wrap her head around it. She was glad that she was marrying Charlie for love.

"What, you don't approve?" Eric asked, seeing her facial expression. "Oh no!"

"Don't be a smartass."

"Why not?"

"Is that your answer for everything?"

"Why not?" he replied and then smirked at her.

"Well, this was a lovely conversation." Stacey turned to leave.

"Hey, wait, you didn't answer me."

She turned to look at him. "About what?"

"The fact that Charlie didn't bring you up at dinner. It didn't bother you?"

"No," she lied.

Eric looked at her closely. She was starting to hate how much he studied her face after every answer she gave.

"Charlie has brought girls home before. They always leave. This time, he changed it up. Proposed to you first. Probably to make it harder for you to leave."

"I'm not leaving," Stacey replied coolly.

He took another drag off his cigarette and said, "We'll see."

Her eyes narrowed. "I guess we will."

She turned around and walked away. Something about the entire conversation had unnerved her. Before Stacey went back into the house, she paused and looked back at Eric. He had turned away from her and was looking up at the moon. The moonlight illuminated his hair and made it look as if he was slightly glowing. She could barely make out the tip of his cigarette, glowing like a cooling ember.

Chapter Five

She dreamt again that night. It had been a while since Stacey had dreamt anything so vivid. After Tina had died, and she had run off to live on Tony's island, her dreams had been dull, as if the color had been drained from them.

Tonight, however, her dream was bright and bold as if a painting had exploded across the wall of her brain. She was walking through the manor, only it was so brightly lit that it felt as if it was a different house all together.

Stacey walked into the kitchen. The marble flooring was replaced with what looked like blood-red tile. Tina sat at the dining room table. She was at the head of the table. A steak was in front of her, which she was slicing very slowly. It didn't even look like it had been cooked. Blood splashed across the plate.

Stacey moved toward her grandmother. She was anxious to touch her again and to hug her. But when she went to do so, Tina suddenly vanished, disappearing into thin air. She turned around, trying to see where her grandmother had gone.

She gasped in surprise. Charlie had startled her. He was standing in the doorway of the dining room.

"Tina. Tina was here," Stacey said to him although her voice sounded far away.

Charlie didn't answer. He just stared at her blankly as if he didn't know her. She went over to him, trying to snap him back into focus but he turned to mist when she got close. Panic started to surge through Stacey. She was afraid that she was never going to get out of here. Where had Tina and Charlie gone?

Someone was laughing behind her. Stacey turned around and saw Eric, sitting where Tina had been just moments before. The sight of him filled her with a rage. He had something to do with them vanishing – she just knew it.

Stacey began to run but Eric just got farther and farther away. She could never get closer to him. He laughed the whole time with a cigarette dangling out of his mouth.

She woke up in a cold sweat and sat up. It took her a few seconds to remember where she was as she looked around the tiny room. The blanket that she had found in the dresser was wrapped around her legs. She yanked it off and took in a deep breath.

The clock on the wall showed it was a little past eight in the morning. Sunlight poked through the blinds. She could hear birds outside. Even though Stacey had slept through the night, she felt exhausted, as if she had run a marathon.

She got out of bed. Her stomach was grumbling, and she wanted to see Charlie. She peeked her head out of the doorway to make sure no one was in the hallway, then went to the bathroom.

After Stacey showered, she decided she'd see if Charlie was awake. They could eat breakfast together and figure out how to tell Terry that Charlie was leaving the business. The manor, like always, was deathly silent.

She walked to the first floor and went to Charlie's room. She knocked twice but there was no answer. She turned the door handle and slowly looked inside. Would it be wrong of her to wake him up?

It didn't matter. His bed was empty. The covers were thrown back as if he had gotten up suddenly. Stacey stood there, feeling a little confused. Where had he gone? She made sure he wasn't in the bathroom before deciding to go look for him.

She wandered into the living room again. Sunlight poured in through the windows which had the curtains pulled back. The room didn't look so scary in the bright sun. It was empty, however. Stacey stuck her head in the kitchen, but no one was there either. She wasn't sure where else to look. She didn't want to get caught creeping around.

As she stood in the kitchen entrance way, debating what to do, Eric strolled in. Stacey closed her eyes briefly, cursing her luck. She really didn't feel like talking to him. Both major interactions she'd had with him had either been based on lies or full of irritation about Charlie.

This morning, he was wearing the same clothes he had been wearing last night. His hair was messy from sleep but his eyes were alert as ever.

"Good morning," he said to her, going over to the coffee maker, "want some coffee?"

She did, but hesitated to ask for some. That meant she would have to stick around with Eric. On the other hand, she could fish around for information about where in the world Charlie had gone.

"While you stand there and debate the coffee conundrum, I'll make some extra," he said when she didn't reply right away.

His back was to her and she fought the urge to flick him off. The more she hung around Eric, the more she understood why Charlie wasn't his brother's biggest fan. He was cocky to a fault and held himself with a composure that just wouldn't seem to crack. He glanced over his shoulder.

"You just going to stand there or what?"

"No, I was going to meet up with Charlie," she lied swiftly.

Eric turned back to the coffee machine and she heard a low chuckle from him, "Were you?"

Something about his tone put her on edge. Stacey had wanted to appear as if she had known where Charlie was, yet now she was getting the sinking feeling that he knew more than she did.

"Yes, that's right."

"Wow, well, you might want to leave now, then. Takes about an hour to get into town. Did you sleep through the alarm or something?"

After saying this, he flicked on the coffee maker and turned to face her. He crossed his arms casually as he leaned against the counter. Stacey could tell that he was trying not to smirk at her, which just made it worse.

"You have no idea where he is, do you?" Eric asked her.

"No, I – I just slept in. That's all."

"Ah, right. So, you're going with Charlie and Dad to check the financials on a company that isn't yours? Sounds logical. On top of that, Dad, who literally pretended you didn't exist last night, is completely okay with this."

Stacey sighed and shrugged. "Fine. You caught me."

Eric rubbed his hands together as if he had discovered a treasure or something equally interesting. "Charlie didn't tell you he was going to town this morning?"

Stacey felt oddly defensive. "He did. I forgot."

The scent of brewing coffee filled the air. Her stomach grumbled loudly. Eric laughed at the noise.

"Want something to eat?"

"Don't you have like, people to cook for you?"

"We do but only Dad calls them. I can make my own eggs, thank you very much," Eric replied, opening the fridge and rummaging around.

Stacey gave up on the idea that she was going to see Charlie this morning and sat down at the breakfast bar. She tried to tell herself that it was fine that he had left without telling her. He probably would have assumed she'd sleep through the entire trip. Nothing to be irritated over.

Eric turned away from the fridge but wasn't holding anything to make for breakfast. He put the objects down on the counter and Stacey raised her eyebrows.

"Isn't it a little early to start drinking?"

"What? That's why the Bloody Mary was invented. So we can drink this early and not be judged," he remarked. "Want one?"

"No thanks."

"Good idea. If Dad saw you drinking this early, he would like you even less."

"But he's fine with you doing it?"

Eric shrugged. "He doesn't care much what I do."

This took Stacey by surprise. From what Charlie had told her, Eric had been scheming to take control of the company his whole life. Surely that would mean that Terry held an interest in what he was up to?

"Eggs are in the fridge," Eric said to her from over his shoulder.

Stacey balked at the idea of cooking in here. The last thing she wanted was for Terry and Charlie to come back while she was cooking and run the risk of Terry making a backhanded comment about her taking liberties in his home. She was clearly not welcomed here at all, let alone allowed to use his kitchen to cook for herself. The coffee maker beeped.

"Your coffee is ready."

"I thought it was yours too," Stacey said.

"Well, now I want a Bloody Mary."

Stacey slid off the stool and went over to the coffee maker. It was some state-of-the-art one with roughly a thousand different buttons and settings. She looked around for where the mugs could be but there were so many cabinets it was impossible to begin to guess.

Eric leaned over and opened the cupboard above the coffee maker to show her where the cups were. Stacey could smell the faint scent of cigarette smoke clinging to his clothes and a thought struck her.

"If he doesn't care what you do, why hide the fact you smoke?"

Eric looked surprised at this. "Really?"

"Yeah."

"Well, because of how my mom died."

Something must have shown on Stacey's face because Eric took a step back and was shaking his head. He mumbled something under his breath. She couldn't catch what he said, but it sounded like *unbelievable*.

"I know she got sick and passed away but…" Stacey trailed off.

"She died of lung cancer. Mom smoked like a chimney. She practically ate cigarettes her entire life. Even after she got diagnosed, Dad said she still kept smoking. That's why I hide it." Eric peered at her. "That's all Charlie told you? That our mom got sick and died? And what, that was enough for you?"

Stacey felt embarrassed. More embarrassed than the rest of the times she had been suffering through that emotion recently. Eric had turned back to making his drink. His shoulders were hunched as if he was holding something in. She silently turned back to the cupboard and pulled down a mug.

"Creamer is in the fridge," he mumbled to her.

"Thanks."

She poured the coffee and went over to the fridge, opening it. It was brimming with all sorts of food and drinks. Stacey leaned forward and looked closer to try to find the creamer.

Suddenly, the door of the fridge was yanked open farther and Eric leaned in. He snatched the creamer off the top shelf and handed it to her.

"Thanks," she repeated lamely.

"I'm not mad at you," he said suddenly to her, "I just don't understand why Charlie didn't tell you how Mom died."

"I should have asked him about her more. He said she got sick and passed away and he looked upset – I didn't want to press him for details."

"Word of advice," Eric said to her, "press Charlie for details or you won't ever find out anything at all."

Stacey opened her mouth to respond when she heard a loud creaking noise from the main hall. It sounded like something breaking in half and it startled her. Eric shot her a grin.

"They're back," was all he said and pulled away from her.

Stacey looked down at the creamer in her hand, trying to steady her beating heart. Eric's advice lingered in her head. It wasn't something she could just throw away. Charlie should have told her how his mother had died. Maybe she *should* have asked him for more details.

Bitter memories swirled to the surface. The fact that he hadn't told her the truth about being a billionaire, and how he hadn't told her about Adele until she had asked. Perhaps there was some truth to Eric's words after all.

Chapter Six

Charlie and Terry entered the kitchen a few moments later. Peter was behind them, positioned almost as if he could catch Terry if he lost his balance. Stacey was over by the counter again, pouring some creamer into her coffee. Next to her, Eric had finished making his drink and was marveling at his work.

"Nice presentation, right?" he said to her and playfully hit her on the shoulder.

She could see Charlie's eyes narrow at the interaction as she turned around to face him.

"What's going on here?" he asked, trying to keep his tone light but failing.

Before Stacey could speak, Eric chimed up, "Your fiancée here woke up early. Guess you forgot to tell her where you were going. Anyway, don't worry. I took good care of her."

"Are you drinking?" Charlie asked him.

"Geez, it's just tomato juice. Loosen up," Eric remarked, walking past Charlie and punching him in the shoulder.

The gesture, similar to the one he had just done to her, was clearly not meant to be playful for Charlie. His fist thudded against Charlie's shoulder. Stacey watched him take a deep breath as Eric slid onto the stool at the breakfast bar.

Stacey decided to take the bull by the horns. She positioned herself in front of Terry and forced a giant smile on her face.

"We made coffee. Would you like some?"

Terry finally looked up at her. Stacey wasn't sure what she was expecting. She was waiting to see how he was going to ignore her this close. He couldn't walk past her from this angle. Maybe he would just yell at her.

Instead, he grunted and shook his head. "No. I don't like coffee."

Then he moved forward as if he was going to run her over. All Stacey could do was flatten herself against the fridge as Peter escorted him through the dining room toward the living room. Stacey and the two brothers watched him leave.

Then she turned to face Charlie. "Look!" she said excitedly. "He acknowledged my existence!"

"Nice one," Eric replied, raising his glass to her.

But Charlie ran his hand over his face. "Please be careful. Don't corner him like that."

Stacey, who had just considered it a personal victory, felt as if someone had stuck a needle in her balloon. "Why not?"

"Cornering him won't endear him to you," Charlie replied.

Eric scoffed. "Nothing she does will endear him to her. He'll accept her once he is either on his deathbed or you two have kids. Doesn't really matter what she does now."

"We don't know that. She could win him over."

"Can you stop talking about me like I'm not in the room?" Stacey snapped, feeling irritated all of a sudden.

Charlie looked alarmed. "We weren't –"

"I wasn't. You were," Eric quipped.

"I was not," Charlie hissed, turning to his brother.

"I'm still here!" Stacey exclaimed.

Charlie turned back to her. "I didn't mean to speak to you like that. I just meant that we should try as best we can to have Dad like you. That's all."

Stacey shook her head. The emotions she had been holding in threatened to bubble over. Eric watched her curiously as if she were an exhibit in the zoo.

"No, your brother is right," she finally said.

Charlie looked alarmed while Eric looked victorious.

"What the hell does that mean?" he asked her.

"Your father isn't going to like me. I could cure cancer and he wouldn't like me. Speaking of cancer," the words rolled off her tongue, hot and venomous, "Thank you for once again making me look like a moron."

She pushed past him before he could stop her. She could hear him asking Eric what he had done. Eric proclaimed his innocence. Stacey walked through the hallway toward the staircase. She wished she could leave. Coming to this place had been a mistake. Charlie was right – his family was messed up. Not only that, but it seemed to bring out the worst in him.

Stacey had made it up the first flight of stairs when she heard Charlie chasing after her. He caught up with her as she reached the second floor. He turned her around and looked at her.

"What's wrong? I don't – listen, Eric told me. That he told you our mother died of lung cancer. But I don't get what you are so upset about."

Stacey let out a dry laugh, "Are you serious?"

"It isn't as if I told you she was still alive or something. I told you – I told you she passed."

"All you said was she got sick and died. You didn't tell me how. And you know what, I didn't ask. I never ask! I just assume you are going to tell me. I don't know why I keep assuming that, because you don't."

"That isn't fair," Charlie protested. "I tell you everything. You can't keep throwing the past in my face. About who I said I was. I thought we moved past that."

"Me too," Stacey said sadly, and she could feel her throat close. "You should just tell me things. Straight up. You didn't tell me you were going to be gone this morning either."

"What? You're upset about that?" His eyes widened in surprise. "I didn't think it was a big deal."

"I woke up and I didn't know where you were. I ran into Eric and he knew. He knew where you were, but not me. It's embarrassing to be kept so little in the loop with you. How can you expect your father to accept me when you won't even tell me where you're going?"

"How are those two things even connected?" Charlie snapped, and Stacey could see that he was bubbling over now as well.

"If you don't think that I am important enough to tell things to, what does that tell your dad? It isn't exactly a vote of confidence!"

"Don't start this. Not now. Not here." He pointed to the floor. "Not while we are in this house."

"You can't tell me what to do. I don't work for you! I am your fiancée! All I'm asking for is to be kept in the loop! Tell me what is going on with you!"

"What is going on with me? Stacey, I am stuck back in this stupid fucking house dealing with my father. My father, who spent the entire morning making jabbing little cutting remarks about what I am doing with my life. And I try to ignore it because I want to tell him gently that I am leaving the company and trying to set out on my own. I want him in the best mood possible for this – I want to be in the best mood possible for this." He was very close to her now, his voice hushed and struggling to remain so. "But that is difficult when I am also dealing with you being upset because I left the house this morning."

Stacey took a step away from him. Her breathing came quickly now as she tried to keep herself in control.

"Oh, well, excuse me! I had no idea that I was here to make sure your mood was stable enough to stand up to your dad! I guess I should be completely okay with you leaving out how your mom died or that you left the house or anything else. Why don't you just do whatever the fuck you want while we're here? Whatever works for you, your royal highness."

Charlie's features colored with anger. "I just assumed you could handle yourself if I left the house for a couple of hours, so excuse me."

"I took care of myself just fine. I'm not a child!" she snapped.

"Well, I'm glad that Eric was there to help you out." His voice was dripping with bitterness and Stacey blinked.

Then she let out a loud bark of laughter. "Are you serious right now? Eric was helping me figure out where the coffee creamer was. Why, are you jealous?"

"I'm not!" he said loudly and then lowered his voice swiftly. "Don't listen to him. Don't even speak to him. He is never up to anything good. He's a liar. Trust me. I know I sound crazy –"

"You do sound crazy."

Charlie ignored her. "He's just a bored kid. He has nothing to do. He just hangs out and causes problems for everyone. Whatever he told you, just ignore it."

"He told me where you were. He told me how your mother died. Both things you failed to tell me yourself," she replied in disgust.

"Fine, if he's so fucking wonderful, go hang out with him then. I'm done with this conversation."

Charlie turned around and began walking down the hallway. Stacey stood there with her mouth slightly open. She couldn't believe that he was *walking away* from her instead of wanting to work things out. Charlie went to his room in a pout like a teenager.

She couldn't remember the last time she had felt so furious. She refused to chase after him. He probably wanted that. Instead, Stacey stormed down the steps back down to the main floor. *Let him sulk in his room then*, she thought to herself.

She cut across the living room and stopped by the kitchen. It was empty. She poured herself a new cup of coffee to replace the one that had cooled down and set off outside.

It was even chillier today. With the sun high up in the sky, Stacey walked toward the gardens. Better to get lost in the fields than deal with anyone from that family. Her heart was pounding in her chest.

Stacey couldn't recall a time she had ever been this angry at Charlie. Even when he had lied about being a billionaire. Even when she had left him because of the craziness with Adele. She had been afraid of being with him – afraid of taking that leap and seeing what would happen. He had always spoken poorly of his family. Now that she was among them, and saw how he acted, she could see why he wanted to run away.

Even so, Stacey didn't think that it excused his behavior. In spite of her best attempts, she did feel as if she didn't exist here. It wasn't a great feeling. She had assumed Charlie would be on her side throughout this. He would defend her and make Terry notice her.

But he hadn't done any of those things. To hear him speak about trying to keep both his mood and Terry's mood intact had angered her. What about her? She was his fiancée. He was supposed to make sure she was okay too, wasn't he?

Stacey looked around. She had wandered into a section of the garden that was a little wild compared to the other areas. There was a bench nearby. She sat down on it and breathed deeply before taking a sip of her coffee. She wondered why this section was untamed. Stacey could ask Charlie – but would he tell her the complete story?

All she wanted was to be kept in the loop on things. She had thought for sure once she got his father to speak to her, it would be a personal victory for the two of them. But he had been irritated with her for even that simple gesture.

Stacey ran her finger over the rim of her coffee cup. Both Eric and Charlie's words floated around in her head, buzzing loudly.

Don't listen to him. Don't even speak to him. He is never up to anything good. He's a liar.

Word of advice. Press Charlie for details or you won't ever find out anything at all.

Hearing the two brothers bicker and insult each other behind their backs suddenly made her miss Allison. It was odd how different her own relationship with her sister had been. Growing up, they had been similar to Charlie and Eric. Yet something had shifted after Tina passed away. Allison had been the one to wake her out of her fog when she had been hiding out on Tony's island.

She slipped her phone out of her pocket and on a whim called Allison. She was sure that she was going to wake her sister up, but she was willing to deal with being snapped at.

"Hey!" Allison answered on the second ring, sounding alarmingly awake for someone who hated getting up before noon.

"Hey. Did I wake you?"

"No, no. I'm up early. I have a flight to catch in an hour. We're going to Belgium for like, three days."

"Wow, Belgium. That should be fun."

"Yeah, I'm excited. I'm on like three cups of coffee already though. Why are you up so early? How awful is it there?"

"How do you know it's awful?"

"Because you're calling me," Allison replied.

Stacey laughed a little shakily. "Yeah. It isn't as great as I thought it'd be."

"I have approximately ten minutes before Jacob gets here. Spill it."

Stacey talked as fast as she could. She told Allison everything from how creepy the manor house was, how Terry ignored her, how Eric had fooled her into thinking he worked here up to the fight she had just had with Charlie. When she finished, she exhaled slowly and waited for Allison to reply.

"Wow, sounds shitty," she finally said.

"Is that all you have to say?" Stacey asked.

"What? What do you want me to say?"

"I don't know. Advice?"

"Well, both you and Charlie need to cool off. Honestly, I wouldn't bother even discussing this stuff until after he tells Terry his news. It's probably weighing really heavily on him. After he tells him and there is the nuclear fallout that will eventually clear, then talk to him. He would be more open to talking and apologizing then, I think."

"Wow," Stacey said, feeling impressed, "when did you get so smart?"

"I think it comes with being married. Soon, you won't need my advice. I have two minutes left. Tell me more about Eric."

"What? Why?"

"He sounds cute."

"Seriously, Allison? You're married."

"Married but not dead," her sister replied solemnly. "Come on. You know I like troublemakers."

"That's because you *are* a troublemaker. I'm going to go now."

"Alright," Allison sighed. "Well, text me later, okay? And don't do anything stupid."

The call ended. Stacey had to admit that she felt a little bit better having vented to Allison. She mulled over her sister's advice. It seemed sound. Charlie was under a lot of stress. Trying to discuss it with him now would only lead to more trouble.

They were here for two more days. Better to just suck it up and deal with it the best that she could.

Chapter Seven

Stacey didn't see Charlie for the rest of the day. She spent most of the day in the garden and once she got bored of that, read a book in one of the sitting rooms in the manor. No one bothered her. She didn't hear anything.

By the time dinner rolled around, her anger had cooled off and had turned into just regular irritation. Peter came to fetch her for the meal. Stacey trailed after him. When she got there, Eric was already there. He was on his phone, typing furiously. Charlie and Terry weren't there yet.

She was about to sit down next to Charlie's seat but not before yanking the place setting that had been set for her three seats down to where he was. Eric glanced up.

"Where were you all day?" he asked.

"One of the thousand sitting rooms this place has."

His phone chimed and he looked back down at it with a roll of his eyes. "Trying to set up a date with this chick and she's making things difficult."

"'Chick?' Really?" Stacey asked, arching an eyebrow.

"Woman. Female. Whatever."

Stacey wasn't interested in his woman problems. She felt on edge, as if she were waiting for the other shoe to drop.

Eric went on, "Anyway. Bad thing about being stuck at this manor is it makes it a bit hard to hook up."

"I don't care," Stacey remarked, glancing over at the doors where Terry had come through last time.

"Wow, you're charming tonight."

"What, like you?"

Eric held his hands up as if he were warding off an attack. "Fight with Charlie, eh?"

She bristled at his comments and looked over at him. "Whatever happened with Charlie isn't any of your business."

That slow, lazy grin moved across his face and he leaned forward as if he were waiting to hear a secret. His phone was on the table now, and it vibrated loudly against the oak table.

"He's jealous, isn't he?"

"Of what?" She played dumb.

"Us. Getting along." He motioned between the two of them.

"Is that what this is? Getting along? It doesn't feel like getting along. Feels more like you talk to me to piss off your brother because the two of you act like children together."

Eric's grin didn't diminish. He didn't get to reply because that was when Charlie entered. His eyes fell on the two of them. Eric was still leaning forward, smiling widely. Stacey could see Charlie's shoulders stiffen at the sight. *Great,* Stacey thought.

He sat down next to her. Eric leaned back in his chair and rubbed his stomach.

"I'm starving," he said.

Neither Stacey nor Charlie replied. Eric picked up his phone and began texting again. The doors opened and Peter came in, helping Terry walk in on his cane. He looked unchanged from this morning. He didn't smile as he sat down.

Instead, he looked over at Eric. "Put your phone away! Every time I see you, you're on that damn thing."

"Sorry, Dad," Eric drawled, shoving the phone into his pocket.

The two same servers came out of the kitchen and put a plate of steak and potatoes in front of everyone. Stacey had a flashback to her dream – Tina, cutting the raw steak, blood pouring out on the plate, and felt her appetite wane.

They began to eat in silence again. Stacey wondered if the meal was going to be as awkward as last night's dinner, when Charlie suddenly cleared his throat.

"I have to tell you something, Dad."

She froze. Eric's eyes fell on her and he squinted at her. He must know she knew whatever Charlie was going to announce. For some reason, she hadn't thought Charlie was going to announce it right now. They still had two days left. She had pictured him mumbling it very quickly as they left.

Terry looked up and grunted, "What?"

Charlie took a deep breath and said the words, "I'm leaving the company. I'm giving up the position of president. I'm walking away."

The reaction was instantaneous. Eric dropped his knife and fork directly onto his plate, looking stunned. Terry practically choked on the piece of steak in his mouth and started coughing. Peter began to hit him on the back. Stacey was concerned he was going to stop breathing.

"Are you serious?" It was Eric who spoke first – Stacey couldn't read the expression on his face.

Terry finally stopped coughing and shook his head. "Don't be stupid, boy."

"I'm not. I'm serious. I should have told you before we went into town today but…" He shook his head. "Anyway, I'm leaving at the end of this quarter. That gives you –"

"Enough!" Terry barked, and he slammed his hand down on the table. "No more of this madness!"

"It isn't madness. I'm leaving, Dad."

But Terry stoutly ignored him by turning to Eric and doing something Stacey hadn't ever seen him do before – ask his son a question. "How was your day?"

Eric's face would have been comical if there hadn't been such a serious thing going on. He cleared his throat but didn't get a chance to reply.

"Dad. Dad, stop. I'm leaving the company. I know you can hear me. Give it to Eric. He's always wanted it, anyway."

Terry turned to look at the two of them. Stacey was reminded of when she was a little girl and had gotten in trouble. Tina used to have the same expression on her face before she grounded her.

But instead of directing his words to Charlie, he looked directly now at Stacey. "Is this your fault?"

"What?" Her throat felt dry at suddenly being put on the spot.

"You heard me. Is this your stupid idea, girl?"

"I'm not a girl," she bristled.

"Listen to me, Charlie. Whatever stupid ideas this one –" and he jabbed his finger toward her, "has put into your head, forget it."

"She didn't put any ideas in my head. You take control of the company then. You were furious you were too sick to run it anyway."

Terry went on as if Charlie hadn't spoken, "This never would have happened if you were marrying Adele."

Charlie slammed the palm of his hand down on the table which made her jump. "But I'm not! I'm not marrying Adele, Dad. I was never going to marry her. I've made that clear over the years. Have her marry Eric if you love her so much."

"Hey, what the fuck? Will you stop doing that?" Eric spoke up now.

"Doing what?"

"Just being like 'Oh, give this shit to Eric, no one cares about him'."

"Not this right now," Charlie snapped. "Feeling badly for yourself so quickly?"

"I'm not feeling badly for myself, just asking for a little human decency from my own brother," he growled back.

Charlie began to shake his head. "No, don't pull that shit."

"What shit?"

"You know exactly what you're doing!" he hissed at his brother.

Eric's muscles tensed. Stacey half expected him to lean over the table and swing at Charlie.

Instead, he said very softly in a controlled voice, "What, just trying to get some respect? I can tell you can't give it. I've spoken to Stacey, you know."

Charlie stood up. So did Eric. They looked like two little boys at the playground about to fist fight over lunch money. The two of them stared each other down. It was Terry who spoke.

"Enough! Both of you! Idiots! Sit back down!" When they didn't move, he exclaimed louder, "Now!"

Charlie took in a slow breath and sat down. The remark that he wasn't treating Stacey with respect seemed to have hit him hard. Eric knew exactly what to say to him to piss him off.

Eric sat down next, crossing his arms. Terry glanced at him before turning to the two of them again.

Charlie cut him off before he could speak. "Stacey didn't even know about this until after I told her. No, listen to me. I don't care if you believe me or not. I'm still leaving at the end of this quarter. I can help you or Eric get things settled. I'm willing to do that."

"Generous," Eric mumbled under his breath.

"Why are you doing this? What brought this on?" Terry demanded.

"I don't want to work here any longer. I'm sick of worrying about you. Worrying about this idiot over here." He gestured to Eric who glowered. "Dealing with you two trying to run it behind my back. I kept fighting you two, but why? I'll leave and start my own thing. It was a matter of pride that kept me here, but I don't care any longer."

"So, you're giving up?" Terry grunted. "I didn't raise you to be a quitter."

"You hardly raised me at all. So just stop, alright? Years and years I've put up with your nonsense and general insanity and for what?"

"Aw, what do you want, boy? Me to tell you that I'm proud of you? Looking for my approval?" Terry sneered at him.

"No, not anymore. Hence why I am leaving." He stood up again. "You two can figure out who is going to take over. If Eric here realizes he can't handle it, maybe you can give it to Adele. We all know you probably want to fuck her anyway, Dad." He dragged out the final word – a slap in the face.

For the first time since Stacey had met him, she saw color fill Terry's face. But Charlie didn't give him a chance to respond. He was already leaving the room. Stacey stood up quickly, not wanting to be alone in the dining room and ran after him.

When they got to the living room, she finally caught up with him and grabbed his arm. "Charlie –"

"No." He shook her off. "I don't want to talk right now."

She felt as if she had been punched in the stomach. All she could do was watch him leave the room. A few seconds later, she heard the front door open and slam shut, leaving her alone in the manor.

Chapter Eight

Stacey heard a knock at her door later on that night and hurried over to answer it. It had been almost six hours since Charlie had stormed out of the house. She had been by the window, straining to see when he was returning.

She had gone up to her room right after Charlie had rebuffed her. She found herself crying, which only made her feel stupid. Was it silly of her to have thought something from their fight earlier would have sunken into that thick skull of his? She had just wanted to be there for him, to lend support to him. The fact that he had rejected her hurt more than Stacey had expected.

So it was with hope that she hurried over to the door and opened it. To her bitter disappointment, it wasn't Charlie, but Eric. The disappointment was so strong she could taste it in her mouth. Stacey fought the urge not to slam the door in his face.

"What?" she asked.

"Charlie back yet?"

"No. You came all this way to ask me that?"

Eric ran his fingers through his hair. "Well, I went to his room first, but it was empty. Thought he might be up here."

"Well, he isn't, so…" She began to push the door shut.

Eric shoved his foot against it, stopping her from closing it. "You knew, right? That he was planning this."

"He told me before he proposed." Eric looked thoughtful at this so she added, "Are we done?"

"Not yet. Want to go for a walk?"

"No. Absolutely not. Not with you, anyway. Can you also stop?"

"Stop what?"

"Don't play innocent with me," Stacey sighed. "Your little jab at Charlie at dinner. About respect and me. Don't think I didn't notice. I'm sick of it. You pretending you know me or how I'm feeling toward him. So just stop."

Eric clicked his tongue against the top of his mouth and shrugged. "But it bothers him so much." He grinned.

"Get out," Stacey said and closed the door firmly.

She waited to hear him leave but he didn't. She could hear him on the other side of the door. Charlie was right – he was annoying.

"Hey, listen, Stace – I can call you that, right? You're going to be my sister-in-law, so… you know," he said through the door.

Stacey didn't say anything. Maybe if she ignored him, he would go away.

"Well, be that way. But tell him that he's making a mistake. He probably hasn't thought this all the way through. You know, because he's an idiot."

In spite of herself, she replied through the door, "How so?"

She could hear him walking away. She cursed inwardly and opened the door. He was strolling down the hallway with his hands shoved into his pockets. His posture was clear – he knew he had hooked her even though she had tried to shut him out.

Stacey hurried after him. For the second time in one night, she was chasing after one of the brothers. It was irritating, to say the least.

"What did you mean by that?"

Eric turned around slowly and feigned surprise as if he hadn't seen her there. "Thought you went to bed."

"Oh, cut the shit, Eric," Stacey snapped. "Tell me what you mean."

"Dad isn't just going to let this slide. He isn't the sort of man who just lets things like this happen. He will crush Charlie and his new business just to prove a point."

"Well, maybe he knows this," she replied uncertainly.

"If he does, then he *is* an idiot. Pulling this shit now. Why?"

"Why not?" she asked, mimicking Eric's own phrase from the night in the garden.

He narrowed his eyes at her and took a step toward her. "You have no idea the shit storm Charlie is leading you into."

"Why do you even care?"

"You're being dumb," he said simply.

Stacey snapped. Before she could stop herself, her hand went flying across his face. She instantly regretted having slapped him. She couldn't recall ever slapping anyone before. She stood there, her hand by her side limply and her breathing coming quickly.

Eric rubbed his cheek idly and regarded her with an expression she couldn't read. He didn't look angry. Stacey wasn't sure what he was feeling.

"Well, you sure showed me," he finally said, and turned to walk down the stairs.

Stacey listened to him go. Somewhere downstairs, a clock chimed midnight. She listened to it count out twelve beats before the manor was shrouded in silence again.

<<<>>>

Someone was shaking her. Stacey groaned softly and twisted in her bed. The shaking got worse. Her eyes fluttered open. Her eyes were still blurry from sleep, so she wasn't quite sure what she was looking at.

Charlie sat beside her on the bed. Surprised, she sat up and looked at him. He appeared exhausted. There were dark circles under his eyes. He was still in the clothes from last night. His hair was messy and he smelled faintly of booze.

"Stacey," he said and cupped her face with his hand. "Hey."

"Charlie? What time is it?"

"Six in the morning."

"Did you just get home? What's going on?"

"We're leaving."

Stacey propped herself up and asked groggily, "What?"

"Yeah. I can't stay here any longer. I'm sorry. I feel like I'm losing my mind. We'll head back to the city early. It'll be better for us."

"What about your dad?"

"Who cares?" he mumbled, standing up.

"No, I mean, with your announcement. He's going to want to discuss things, right?"

"There isn't anything to discuss. He can decide who is going to replace me and I'll help them settle in with things. Even if it's Eric."

At the mention of Eric, memories flickered across her mind. She saw him warning her about Terry. She recalled the way she had slapped him and his final words to her as he walked away. She wanted to apologize for the way she reacted but there apparently wasn't going to be any time.

"Come on. Pack up. We're leaving in an hour," Charlie said and left the room, closing the door behind him.

Stacey sat there in bed. Charlie had still been distant. Sure, they were leaving, which was a good thing. But she couldn't help but think they were leaving on a bad note with everyone involved.

There had been no good-bye to Terry or Eric. They had left an hour later, packed and driven to the airport in silence. Charlie had the radio on, making it clear that he didn't want to talk. Stacey wanted to reach out to him and talk to him, but she was too afraid of being rebuffed.

Even though she was making her best attempt at not stressing out, it was failing. She felt as if Charlie was drifting away and she was trying to catch up. When he had told her he was going to talk to his father about leaving, she had been picturing something completely different. There had been no fights in that scenario. Just the two of them working together and facing down his father.

On the plane ride home, Charlie slept. Yet another chance for them to speak was gone. What if he didn't want to discuss it at all? What would she do then? She watched him sleep, her heart aching at the fear that she should have stuck with her choice. The choice she made that day in the graveyard at Tina's funeral, when she had shut the world out, and decided to shut down her feelings for Charlie.

She had been afraid to take that leap with him. Afraid of getting her heart broken. If that ended up actually happening now, Stacey wasn't sure what she was going to do.

A car was waiting for them at the airport. Charlie was on his phone, checking e-mails and tending to business. Stacey idly thought about William and the real estate office. She would be happy to go back to it. It would give her something to focus on.

"Stacey," Charlie's voice came through her fog and she turned to look at him. "Did you hear me?"

"No. I'm sorry. What is it?"

"Do you want to come home with me first?"

The offer took her by surprise, but she nodded that she did. She had been expecting him to drop her off at her place without another word. Charlie seemed to be relieved that she had agreed with him.

By the time they got to the penthouse, Stacey felt exhausted. It was nice to be back in the city. It felt as if she were back on solid ground. The manor, besides being creepy and odd, seemed to have brought out the worst in everyone. She was glad that she was back home.

Charlie dropped his bags to the floor and yawned, "Man, I am tired."

"Me too."

"Last few days sucked."

"They sure did," Stacey replied.

Charlie stared at her for a beat and then threw himself down on the couch, "I'm sorry."

Stacey looked over at him in shock. Her sister had been right. Once he was free of that atmosphere, he was open to talk. Feeling boosted by this, she went over and sat down next to him on the couch.

"I'm sorry too," she said. "I didn't mean to piss you off or make you feel cornered."

He waved his hand. "Don't worry about it. I should have stuck up for you more. I should have made Dad take notice of you. I thought I wasn't rocking the boat but honestly, I was letting him control me. I always do that."

"I get it. Your dad is…"

"Believe me, I've heard it all before," Charlie mumbled.

"That must have been hard. Growing up with that, I mean."

He sighed, "It wasn't fun. I don't mean to sound like 'oh, poor rich kid, woe is me' or anything. But Dad wasn't kind. Like I said before, when Mom died it was as if all the kindness was sucked right out of him. He wanted me to be groomed for the company and that was all he cared about."

"Do you think Eric will take it over?" Stacey asked thoughtfully.

"I don't know. I would assume so, yes. He's always wanted to. Let him have it."

"You know…" She hesitated for a moment. She wanted to tell him what Eric had said but didn't want to upset Charlie by letting him know that Eric had come to her room.

"What?" he asked her. "Why do you look funny?"

"Sorry. Just tired," she said swiftly. "I don't remember what I was going to say."

She should have just told him. But Charlie seemed extremely sensitive about Eric. She had bickered with Eric as if he was her own brother, yet Charlie didn't see it that way. He thought the worst of him – most likely for good reason. If she told him that Eric had told her Terry was going to have it out for him, he would probably be upset. Maybe even angry with her for not mentioning it sooner.

On top of that, she had slapped Eric. Stacey still felt guilty about it. No, better not to let Charlie know. He had probably accounted for Terry's anger, anyway.

"Come here," he said and pulled her toward him.

She went willingly, draping her arms around his neck and bringing her lips to his. It was nice feeling him like this – no more anger or awkwardness between the two of them.

"I'll be honest with you. I'm sorry," he whispered against her neck. "I don't even realize I'm doing it."

He left butterfly kisses down her neck and Stacey closed her eyes. "It's okay. Families always bring out the worst in people."

Charlie chuckled. "They sure do. But we don't have to worry about it any longer."

Being back home with just Charlie felt nice and relaxing. The tensions of dealing with the family seemed to have faded into the background. For a while, they did nothing but watch TV. Stacey had her head on his shoulder as they flipped through the channels together. Stacey even dozed off at one point, finally able to unwind a little.

When she woke up, she let out a yawn and looked up. She was curled against Charlie who looked down at her and smiled.

"Sleep well?"

"Yeah, I needed that," she replied, sitting up and turning to face him. "Did I miss anything exciting?"

Charlie shook his head and grinned, "No, but you look cute sleeping."

Stacey laughed and he leaned forward to kiss her. His hands trailed down her sides. He slid his hand down her pants and ran a finger down the front of her underwear, causing her to shiver.

His lips found hers and he tugged on her bottom lip, whispering, "We don't have to worry about anything."

He moved her underwear to the side. His fingers were cold against the heat of her body. She tingled all over as Charlie gently probed her pussy with his finger. She buried her face in his shoulder, closing her eyes.

Very slowly, his finger entered her. She was already wet. The smallest touch from Charlie made her melt. His finger moved deep inside of her, promising her more, but making her wait for it.

Then another finger slipped into her pussy. Stacey's grip on his shoulders tightened as Charlie began to move them in and out quickly. His other hand was on the small of her back, holding her in place. Stacey grinded her hips against his fingers, wanting more.

Charlie pulled his fingers out of her and then moved them to her mouth. She wrapped her lips around them, rolling her tongue around his fingertips. He watched her with his eyes wide. His mouth was slightly parted as if he was in the middle of a gasp.

Then he pulled her clothes off. Stacey yanked his clothes off just as urgently. When their bare skin finally touched, she was in ecstasy.

Charlie leaned against the couch and pulled her toward him. She moved into his lap. His cock pressed against her now. She could feel it throbbing. He cradled the back of her neck and their lips met. This kiss was feverish with desire, an urgency that hadn't been in their lovemaking in quite some time.

If the manor had worked to crush what they had, being out of it and back home was bringing it all back to life. Stacey could feel herself blooming under every touch of Charlie's. She could feel every detail of him – his fingertips pressed against the back of her neck, his tongue in her mouth, his heart racing against her own.

With his free hand, he positioned himself so he could enter her. Stacey held onto him as his cock slipped into her pussy. She moaned into his mouth as she felt him fill her up with his dick. With his tongue still in her mouth, Charlie leaned back and let her ride him.

Stacey rocked her hips at first, getting used to how he filled her from that angle. She felt stuffed, as if he had taken her completely over. His mouth moved to her breasts, biting and tugging on her nipples. She threw her head back and began to pick up speed.

The sound of their skin smacking together filled the room. Charlie cupped her breasts and buried his face in them as she brought her hips down on his cock again and again.

"You look so good," he said between gasps for air as she fucked him on the couch.

Stacey couldn't reply. Her body felt frozen as if every nerve in her body was vibrating. From this angle, he felt incredible. His dick was warm and hard inside of her. Her pussy accepted every inch of him. She could feel herself on the verge.

Charlie gripped her hips so hard that Stacey couldn't moan anymore. Her eyes fluttered open.

"What are you doing?" she asked dizzily.

"This." He moved her so they were almost falling off the couch onto the floor.

Before she could say anything, Charlie's head was in between her legs. He buried his tongue deep in her pussy and flicked it out to her clit. Stacey let out a moan of surprise, rolling her head back against the floor. Behind her, she could see the city spread out like a jewel. Upside down, dizzy with pleasure, it looked full of possibilities. She felt like a queen in a tower.

Charlie's tongue rolled across her clit before darting back down the length of her pussy. His face pressed against her as she shuddered and rolled her hips against him. She was going to finish – she was going to come right now.

As if sensing this, he was suddenly gone. Stacey let out a groan of frustration from having been on the brink both times. Her eyes had been closed and when she opened them, Charlie was on his knees next to her. His dick was hard in her face, dripping with pre-cum.

"Suck it," he ordered huskily.

Stacey obeyed, rolling over onto her stomach and engulfing him with her mouth. His cock was warm and twitching in her mouth as she lapped at it with her tongue. She gripped his dick at the base with one hand. She covered it in her spit before bobbing her head up and down on his thick shaft.

Charlie groaned and shut his eyes. Stacey took as much of him as she could in her mouth until he hit the back of her throat. Then it popped out of her mouth, slick with her spit. She jacked him off with her hand before taking him in her mouth again.

He grunted and pulled away. He pushed her onto the floor and climbed on top of her. Without pausing, he entered her fluidly. He began to fuck her hard and fast on the floor. Her body shook with each thrust, her tits jiggling as he fucked her.

It didn't take long to finish. They were both so close. After a few thrusts, Stacey's orgasm exploded over her. She arched her back and let out a loud guttural moan as she came. Charlie came at the same time, grunting and breathing hard. She had her legs wrapped around his waist as she came.

After it was done, he collapsed on top of her. They were both sticky with sweat and the air smelled of sex. Stacey gasped for breath. Her body felt numb, although her scalp was still tingling from the remnants of her orgasm.

He kissed her gently before rolling off of her. They lay on the floor as if they had both melted there. She turned her head and smiled at him.

Everything felt okay now.

Chapter Nine

The next two weeks went by in a blur of activity. Stacey threw herself into helping William, Amanda, and Brad set up the real estate office. On top of that, she was helping William figure out repairs on her own building.

She was so busy that everything else seemed to fade into the background. She would get up early, work late into the night, and come home to fall asleep. Charlie had to go to Europe for a business trip the second week. Part of her wanted to go with him but she refused to leave William hanging. He had been kind enough to give her time off to go meet Charlie's family. She didn't want to ask for more time off.

Stacey had learned a lot during her time with Tony. It had been easy to slip into a role she didn't even realize she was falling into. She had been comfortable with him paying for things, and she had allowed herself to ruin a job just to run away with him.

It was going to be different with William. This was a chance to build an office from the ground up. Stacey didn't want to blow it. She said good-bye to Charlie at the airport and then went back to work.

It wasn't until one night when she was staying late that Amanda poked her head into the room. Their office was small and on the outskirts of the city. They could have gotten someplace nicer, but William wanted to start small. Stacey couldn't blame him. There was a chance this could all go under. Amanda had been taking classes to get her real estate license in the meantime, so they would have at least one agent in the office.

"You're still here?" Amanda had said.

Stacey looked up. "Yeah. Just finishing up some things. Why are you here?"

"I left my phone here before I went to class." She held her phone up as if it were proof. "Had to come back to get it."

"Aren't you overwhelmed?" Stacey asked. "You're taking college courses on top of real estate courses and popping by here."

Amanda sat at the edge of the desk that William had put in the room earlier today, "Massively, stupidly busy. But I don't mind. I hate being idle."

"Well, don't overdo it."

"You either," Amanda crossed her arms. "Don't you have a wedding to plan?"

"We haven't set a date yet."

"Why not?"

Stacey paused and then shrugged, "Just haven't."

"What's the hold-up? You guys are clearly in love. Just hire a planner and be done with it."

"I hadn't thought about it before."

To be honest, Stacey hadn't been thinking about the wedding much lately. Between dealing with Charlie's family and being busy with work, the wedding had been something in the back of her mind. Both she and Charlie had such busy schedules that planning a wedding had felt daunting.

A planner, however…

"I'll talk to Charlie about it."

Amanda clapped her hands together. "Great! I'm expecting the largest wedding I've ever attended. Don't let me down," she joked as she waved good-bye.

The largest wedding I've ever attended. Something about those words left Stacey feeling uneasy. She just couldn't put her finger on it.

"Meredith is supposed to be the best," Charlie reminded her as they walked into the building. "She organized a couple of my friends' weddings and they were crazy. Ice sculptures, for one."

"Ice sculptures?" Stacey asked, balking at the idea.

Something must have shown on her face because he quickly amended with, "We don't need those though."

After Charlie had gotten back into town, Stacey had told him about the wedding planner idea. He was thrilled and promptly set up a meeting. She wasn't sure what to expect. This was a whole new arena for her. Most things in her relationship with Charlie were like that.

The office was on the first floor. The waiting room looked more like a living room, with a large couch and TV. They were offered freshly brewed coffee as they waited. After five minutes, the door on the other end of the room opened and a woman burst out of it.

"Charlie!" she trilled. "I can't believe you're getting married!"

"Meredith," Charlie smiled, standing up.

Stacey got a good look at Meredith, apparently the golden girl of wedding planning. She was rail thin and tottering on four-inch-high heels. She was also a lot older than Stacey had been expecting, seeing as her hair was completely white and skin wrinkled in places. Her face was frozen, as if she had injected more Botox in it than necessary, especially since there were still deep lines around her mouth. On top of that, she was a hideous shade of orange, as if she lived for fake tanning.

"Is this the woman who stole your heart?" Meredith cooed, turning to Stacey.

"The one and only," Charlie said, gently shoving her forward.

She stuck out her hand toward Stacey. There were massive rings on each finger, all of them sparkling under the lights of the office. She shook Meredith's hand, which was freezing cold.

"Great. Amazing. Wonderful," she kept adding on adjectives as her eyes raked over Stacey.

She felt exposed in front of this woman, even though Meredith looked ridiculous. Stacey was now hyper aware of her size next to how freakishly skinny this woman was. She pushed her concerns to the side. Now was not the time to let them get to her.

"Come on back to my office, darling, we must speak," she said, resting her hand on Stacey's shoulder and steering her down the hallway as if she were a car.

She glanced behind her to see Charlie following. He wore a bemused expression on his face as if he was getting a kick out of all of this. They went into the first room. The windows had the blinds raised up, allowing them to see the view of the river that cut through the city.

On the walls were photographs of happily married couples. There were fresh flowers on the desk, filling the room with a pleasant scent. Stacey and Charlie sat down on the opposite side of the desk as Meredith held a tablet in her perfectly manicured hands.

"Okay, hit me. What are you thinking? What do you envision?" She swept one of her hands in the air and the bangles on her arm jangled loudly.

Stacey glanced at Charlie who spoke first.

"Well, we don't have anything particular in mind. We don't even have a date set."

Meredith drummed her fingernails against her desk. They were long and fake, making clickity noises that sounded like a typewriter. She glanced at a calendar.

"Have you thought about a winter wedding?"

"That's really close," Stacey remarked. "Is that even possible?"

Meredith laughed loudly, as if Stacey had said something very funny. "Dear, I can make anything possible. What about January? Holidays are over. Everyone is winding down. It'd be nice then." She had already turned her attention to her tablet, swiping her bony fingers across the screen.

Charlie looked at her and asked, "What do you think?"

Stacey wasn't sure what to think. To be honest, the entire thing was a bit overwhelming.

"I can get you January twentieth at the House Gardens," Meredith declared.

"House Gardens?" Stacey asked.

Meredith lowered the tablet and smiled at the two of them. "I like this girl." She pointed at Stacey as if she was declaring something. "She's cute. She's fresh."

Even though it was a compliment, it felt more as if she were being called cute for not understanding what the House Gardens was.

Charlie cleared his throat and said, "The House Gardens is about an hour away. It's a lush estate filled with flowers and amazing landscapes. It's a hotel. A retreat."

"An hour away?" Stacey asked, thinking about the logistics of having a wedding there.

Meredith slid the tablet across the desk and tapped her finger on the screen, "Look, look!"

Stacey did. The screen was full of images. She gingerly held the tablet and looked at them. The estate was old fashioned, like something out of a novel. It looked faintly like the manor that Terry lived in, only draped in bright colors surrounded by beautiful vivid grounds. The images of the gardens were especially striking. All sorts of different flowers and plants sprawled across it. There was also a view of the ocean, twinkling like a gem.

"Wow," she said and meant it – it was stunning.

Meredith rattled on, "Make a weekend of it. The estate can only hold three hundred guests, however, so we will have to trim the guest list."

She froze and looked up, "Three hundred?"

Meredith pouted, looking childish for a woman her age. "Ah, I know it will be hard. But I think we can manage it."

"No, no, I mean – we aren't inviting three hundred people. We aren't going to be even close to that," Stacey remarked, turning to look at Charlie.

He didn't reply. He was looking at her a bit uncomfortably before he finally said, "How many were you thinking?"

"I don't know." She began to mentally count on her fingers. "Maybe like twenty?"

"Twenty?" Charlie exclaimed at the same time Meredith did.

"Yeah, why?" She looked at the two of them, confused. "Charlie… how many were you expecting?"

"I had it pegged for around two hundred and fifty to three hundred," he admitted.

This time it was Stacey's turn to exclaim. Meredith swept the tablet out of her hands and smiled at them.

"My, my, lots to discuss! I'm sure you two will agree on a guest list! The House Gardens then?"

Charlie looked at Stacey, who wasn't sure what to say. She couldn't imagine having that many people attending their wedding. Meredith, sensing the mood change, stood up.

"Excuse me for a moment," she said politely and shut the office door behind her.

"Charlie, that is way too many people," Stacey said as soon as the door closed. "I don't even know that many people."

"It'll just be business people mostly. Especially since I am starting the investment firm. Inviting them to our wedding would be prudent."

She scowled. "Our wedding shouldn't be about business deals."

"No, no, that isn't what I meant," he said hastily. "I just meant that I think everyone being involved would be good all around. You can invite anyone you want too."

"That's like five or six people," Stacey protested. "So, what, two hundred and forty-five of them will be for you?"

"You have distant family though. Cousins."

"That I haven't spoken to in years!"

Charlie reached for her hand and looked her in the eyes. "I know it's a big deal. January is soon and it's a bit daunting to think it's coming that quickly. But I want to give you the best. Including a big wedding. We'll cut it down. A hundred people, tops."

"That's a bit better," she said, feeling her will start to give.

Charlie smiled. "Perfect. I'll just figure out who to not invite."

"Your brother," she joked, and Charlie cracked a smile.

As if she knew the topic had been resolved, the office door opened and Meredith breezed into the room. She sat behind the desk and smiled brightly.

"All set?"

"Yes," Stacey said firmly. "Book the House Gardens."

"Perfect!" Meredith trilled.

Charlie met her eyes and smiled.

Chapter Ten

When they got back to Charlie's penthouse, Stacey was in a good mood. She had felt overwhelmed by the wedding plans when she had first met Meredith, but at least now it was being taken care of by someone who knew what they were doing. The House Gardens was beautiful. Even though the guest list was still too large, she could deal with it. It was still going to be their special day, no matter what.

Charlie had been saying as much as they walked into the living room. It was Stacey who saw Eric first. He was in the living room, flopped down on the couch, making himself at home. The TV was on but muted, and he was flipping through the channels at a rapid rate.

"Charlie… Charlie." She had to say it twice to get him to stop talking and look to where she was pointing.

He turned around and stared at Eric on the couch. Eric stopped flipping channels. He had a bag of chips in his lap, and had shoved a handful into his mouth as he waved at them with his free hand.

"What the fuck are you doing in here?" Charlie demanded.

"Whoa," Eric said through a mouthful of chips, "Is that any way to greet your brother?"

Charlie stalked over to the couch and yanked the bag of chips out of Eric's hands. He protested as Charlie tossed them on the coffee table.

"Why are you here?" he asked again.

Eric swallowed the chips. "What do you mean? You invited me."

Charlie's brow furrowed. "No, I didn't."

"Yeah, you did. Remember, when you told Dad you were leaving the company? You said you'd train anyone who was taking over. Well, you're looking at him."

Stacey heard Charlie scoff before replying, "I was hoping Dad was actually going to pick someone capable to run it."

Eric ignored the jab and turned his head to look at Stacey. She felt her insides twist a little at the sight of him. She could recall the slap she had given him and his last words. *Well, you sure showed me.*

"Hey there, future sister-in-law."

"Eric," she said with a slight nod of her head.

"Get out. Get a hotel. You aren't staying here."

"Dad said I have to."

"I don't care," Charlie snapped, "You're not staying here."

"Why, too cramped for three people?"

"Stacey doesn't live here, but anywhere with you is too cramped."

"Wait, wait, wait," Eric said, holding his hands up. "Stacey doesn't live here?"

Already sensing where this was going, she quickly walked forward. "There's that hotel down the street. Eric could stay there."

"I told you already. Dad said I have to stay here."

"And I told you that I don't care. So get your shit and go."

"That really hurts." He rested his hand on his heart. "That hurts deeply."

Charlie rolled his eyes. Eric suddenly showing up wasn't good for anyone, Stacey thought to herself. It was going to put Charlie on edge. Why did Eric have to appear now?

"How did you get in here anyway?" Stacey asked him.

"Dad has a key."

"For emergencies," Charlie added, "not so you could come in here and eat my chips."

"They were almost stale. I was doing you a favor."

"Out. Hotel down the street. Take it up with Dad if you don't like it."

Eric shrugged. "If you want. Don't know why you'd want to piss him off more though."

"Don't care," Charlie snapped, brushing his words aside. "I'm going to change. I want you gone by the time I'm done. We will discuss training at another time."

He stalked out of the room, leaving Stacey alone with Eric. He was getting to his feet, brushing crumbs off his shirt. He wore a baggy t-shirt and jeans with holes in them. Stacey couldn't imagine Charlie ever wearing such an ensemble.

He picked up a backpack and slung it over his shoulder.

"Is that all you brought?" she asked, not wanting to have any silence in between the two of them.

"Yeah. I can just buy whatever I need when I have to so…" he shrugged.

He started walking down the hallway. Stacey watched him go, then propelled herself forward toward him. Her fingers wrapped around the sleeve of his grungy t-shirt and yanked gently. Eric paused and looked over his shoulder.

"I'm sorry. For slapping you. I didn't get a chance to apologize."

For a few seconds, Stacey wondered if he was going to lecture her or tell her he was mad at her. She didn't want to make things worse between members of Charlie's family.

But then that lazy grin swept across Eric's face. "Worried, Stace?"

"It was wrong to slap you, but don't tempt me to do it again," she said firmly.

"Sure. Whatever you say," his grin only got wider and he leaned forward, bringing his voice down to a whisper, "I forgive you though."

The bedroom door slammed shut and Stacey took a step away from him.

"I better leave before I get in trouble," he said, turning around with a wave and heading toward the front door.

Charlie came out and stood next to Stacey, watching his brother depart. Once Eric was gone, Charlie sighed heavily.

"What the hell?" he mumbled.

Stacey turned to him. "Don't let him bother you. He knows all your weak points. I'm sure your dad sent him here just to bother you. Throw you off your game."

Charlie ran his hand over his face. "Probably. Just what I need right now."

"We can handle Eric. Together." She laced her fingers through his and smiled brightly.

He returned the smile. "You're right. Hey, we aren't at the manor. So we can handle it however we want."

"Exactly."

Charlie pulled her in for a kiss and all thoughts of Eric were quickly forgotten.

Chapter Eleven

Allison was coming over to meet Meredith and help plan some of the wedding details. She had put together that beautiful wedding on Tony's island, after all, and was better at this sort of thing. It was a no-brainer for Stacey to make her sister the maid of honor.

Meredith was meeting them at Charlie's place. He was still at the office, trying to finish up in order to make the meeting, although Stacey doubted that would be possible. At least Allison would be there. Meredith was slightly weird, and that unnerved Stacey. She knew that her sister would help make her feel more secure with any choices she made.

This was the first time Stacey had been here alone in Charlie's place. She had wandered through it, feeling a little like a ghost. Something was bothering her, although she couldn't quite put her finger on it. It was as if there were a small bud of anxiety in her chest, waiting to bloom.

By the time she sat down to get ready for Meredith, Stacey felt oddly jittery, as if she had drank two coffees one after another. She heard the elevator emit a soft ding and stood up, brushing her skirt smooth.

But it was Eric who waltzed into the room, not Meredith. Stacey tried to keep the scowl off her face. She was determined to have the two brothers eventually patch things up. If she had to play peacemaker between them, she couldn't lob insults at him as casually as Eric did to everyone else.

"Eric!" she exclaimed stiffly. "What are you doing here?"

"Nice to see you too, Stace." He drawled on the nickname he had given her before cutting into the kitchen.

She trailed after him. He had opened the fridge and was rummaging around in it as if he lived here. Like the other day, Eric was dressed down, looking like he was going to spend all day playing video games instead of training for a job.

"Ah, there it is," he said from behind the fridge door and then poked his head out, dangling a can of iced coffee.

"You came all this way for an iced coffee?"

He shut the fridge door. "No. Charlie told me to meet him here."

"I have a meeting with the wedding planner in like, ten minutes here," Stacey said urgently.

"What, am I not allowed to see her or something? I might woo her over with my charms."

For someone who wasn't handsome and who easily looked older than Charlie by ten years, Eric sure was cocky.

"Somehow, I don't think she's your type," Stacey replied, going back into the dining room.

Eric opened up the can of iced coffee and took a swig. "Well, I'll stick around, anyway."

"Don't. My sister is coming by to help."

"She the one that married Jacob?" When Stacey nodded, he went on, "Man. Imagine being married to that guy. Talking to him is like watching paint dry. I would rather sit through a lecture from my dad than have to talk to Jacob."

"He's a good guy. Just a little dry."

"That's putting it mildly. He's like taking a depressant. I'm going to assume your sister is with him for the money or something like that."

Stacey looked over at him, alarmed. Even though it was true, she wasn't exactly comfortable with everyone guessing that so easily. Eric saw her face and let out a laugh.

"Don't worry. I'm sure no one else knows."

"How did you?" she asked slowly.

"Previous experience," was all he said when the elevator dinged again.

Stacey quickly excused herself and walked over to the foyer. Allison was there, dressed in a sleek purple pantsuit. Stacey couldn't recall ever seeing her sister wearing one of those before. Her hair was pulled up in a high ponytail and draped over one of her shoulders like a sleek curtain.

"Hey," she said to Allison and lowered her voice, "Charlie is going to try to make it. His brother is here."

Allison's eyebrows raised. "The one that everyone dislikes?"

"Yeah. He said he's waiting for Charlie, I guess. Listen, play nice, okay?"

"Play nice? Am I ten?"

Stacey cast a glance in the direction of where Eric was and replied, "No but he has a way of annoying everyone he comes in contact with."

"Sounds great to me. I love troublemakers."

She breezed past Stacey, leaving a trail of perfume wafting behind her as she went into the dining room. Stacey followed.

Eric was sitting at the dining room table, flipping through some of the wedding materials that had been strewn across it. He was looking at each one intently, as if any part of this wedding had anything to do with him.

He looked up and stopped when he saw Allison. He straightened in his chair and smiled at her easily. "You must be Meredith," he said in a tone of voice that Stacey had never heard from him before.

Of course, Stacey sighed inwardly. At first glance, most people didn't think Allison and Stacey looked related. The truth was most people couldn't see past their size difference. If they had, they would have seen that both sisters shared the same button nose and wide eyes. But Eric, clearly already thinking with his dick, wasn't interested in looking for any sort of family resemblance.

Allison sat down on one side of the table and flipped open one of the wedding magazines. She glanced up at him and replied simply with a "No."

Eric's gaze flicked between Allison and then back to Stacey. She could see it finally click. He leaned back in his chair and took a sip of his coffee.

"Of course. You must be Allison."

"That's right. And you're Eric. Heard a lot about you."

"Is that so? Good things, I hope," he said lazily, his gaze still fixed on Allison as if he was determined to flirt his way into a longer conversation with her.

"Not really," Allison quipped and then turned to Stacey. "Have you thought about a dress?"

Stacey risked a glance over at Eric who had turned his attention back to a magazine about flower arrangements, and then answered her sister, "Not really."

"You need to. This wedding is happening quickly. You need to make plans fast. I know you like to take your time, but big choices have to be made right away," her sister lectured.

That strange feeling was swooping over Stacey again. She clutched her stomach and swayed on her feet for a few seconds. Eric noticed first, and he squinted at her.

"Are you okay?"

"I think I'm going to be sick," she mumbled before taking off down the hallway.

There was a guest bathroom here. She pushed open the door and aimed her head over the toilet. Nothing happened. Stacey sunk to her knees, clutching the side of the bowl. Her knuckles were white from gripping it and she closed her eyes.

"Stacey?" her sister's voice rang out.

Stacey couldn't answer, afraid if she opened her mouth that she would start to throw up. Allison knocked on the door and then slowly opened it. When she saw Stacey with her head over the bowl, she sunk to the floor next to her and began to rub her back.

"Hey, whoa, are you alright?"

"Just feel sick. I thought I was going to throw up. Sorry, I'm fine," Stacey mumbled.

In the distance, she heard the elevator ding and tried to move. But Allison's hands were firmly on her.

"Eric can handle it," Allison said.

The thought of leaving Eric alone with Meredith wasn't exactly filling her with joy but she had no choice. Her sister got to her feet and went over to the sink. A few seconds later, she came back with a cup of water.

"Here, take a sip."

Stacey moved away from the toilet and pressed her back against wall. The tile was cold against her legs although she could feel a thin layer of sweat on the back of her neck. She took the cup from Allison and gulped it down. Allison got her more and handed it to her, warning her to sip this one.

Stacey did. She could hear mumbled voices – Meredith's high pitch, mile a minute voice and the low rumble from Eric.

After she finished the second cup of water, the sick feeling had mostly dissipated. Stacey exhaled slowly and handed the cup to a concerned looking Allison.

"I'm okay. I've been feeling off all day."

"Stress, I'm sure. You're probably overthinking this entire wedding."

"Yeah," she mumbled back, not wanting to go into how stressed she truly was.

Allison brushed a lock of hair from her face. The gesture was small but touched her anyway. It was just more proof of how much their relationship had changed over the last few months.

"Come on," she said to Stacey. "Let's go make sure Eric hasn't done anything awful."

"I thought you said he could handle it," Stacey replied, alarmed.

"Not sure what Eric could handle to be honest," Allison said and stood up, offering her hand to Stacey.

She took it, getting to her feet. The two of them headed toward the dining room.

Chapter Twelve

Stacey wasn't sure what she was expecting when she went into the dining room. Meredith looking horrified, perhaps, at having to talk to Eric for so long.

She certainly hadn't been expecting the two of them to be talking in front of the dining room table. They were standing close together. Meredith was twirling a lock of her vividly white hair and was laughing loudly. Eric was joking about something. When he finished, she laughed again and rested her hand on his shoulder.

He saw them first and looked at Stacey with the sort of expression on his face that said *what did you expect me to do*?

"Meredith, I'm so sorry for the delay," Stacey said, stepping in between them before Meredith could tackle Eric to the floor.

"I was sick," Allison lied swiftly. "My fault. I'm sorry."

Meredith, who had looked irritated at Stacey being late, suddenly softened when Allison blamed herself. She rested her hand on Stacey's shoulder.

"Things happen! Normally, I cannot stand anything off schedule but when family comes into play, what can you do!" she said loudly, a bright smile plastered on her face.

"Yes, of course," Stacey replied although she didn't know why it mattered if she were sick or her sister.

Somehow Allison had known though. She looked over at her sister who only shrugged. She would ask her later.

"Would you like something to drink?" Stacey asked Meredith, who was back to staring at Eric.

"Yes, please. Some water would be lovely."

"I'll help," Eric said quickly, using the opportunity to get a break from Meredith and her man-eating grin.

He followed Stacey into the kitchen. She turned to look at him and couldn't help but ask, "What the hell was that about?"

"Allison said to distract her," Eric said in a low voice. "She said Meredith drops clients all the time for the smallest things because she's super picky. If you were late, even if you were sick, Allison said Meredith would be extremely put off and drop you as a client. She sounds unreasonable as hell. Charlie really thought she'd be good for your wedding?"

Before this could turn into an anti-Charlie rant, she interrupted him, "I was maybe three minutes late."

"Ask your sister. I don't know. Anyway, I just started flirting." He shrugged, as if this made sense.

"Well, she seems super into you now."

"Can't blame her," he said as he opened the fridge to pull out bottles of water. "I'll just have to ward her off, I guess."

"Good luck with that."

"Are you sure you trust a woman so orange she looks like one of those cheese puffs to plan your wedding?" Eric suddenly asked her.

"She comes highly recommended," Stacey said defensively.

"Doesn't mean she's the right fit for you," Eric said and looked at her for a long moment before adding, "Come on. Wouldn't want to make her wait any longer."

He turned and left the kitchen. Stacey watched him leave, that queasy feeling back in her stomach. As much as she hated to admit it, Eric had a point.

By the time Meredith left, Stacey had a gigantic headache. It felt as if a tornado had swept through the dining room. The table was covered with plans and other ideas. There was a guest list in the middle of the table that was close to 300 people. Meredith had been trying to convince her to do a fireworks show, which Allison swooped in and put an end to after seeing how annoyed Stacey was getting.

Even though the fireworks show was off the table, there were still tons of other things that felt as if they were being planned with hardly any input from her. When Meredith left, Stacey sat there, feeling dazed. She could hardly recall everything that had been planned.

Allison came back into the room from the foyer. "Guess we should clean some of this shit up."

"Guess so."

Eric followed in after her sister. "She asked for my number! Can you believe that?"

"Wow, you have a suitor," Allison replied.

He ran his hand over his face – a gesture that Charlie did regularly. At the memory of him, Stacey looked around the room. He hadn't shown up. She had been expecting that he wasn't going to be able to make it. Even so, she felt a kernel of disappointment in her chest. He was the one who had wanted this many guests, after all. If he had been here, maybe Meredith would have been more likely to listen to them about how they had agreed to trim it down.

"Not a suitor I want," Eric grumbled.

"Stacey, you should go lie down," Allison said, ignoring Eric, "you look awful."

She nodded numbly and got to her feet, "Yeah, I still don't feel a hundred percent."

"Eric and I will clean up. Go lie down."

Too tired, with a headache too strong to protest, Stacey nodded and headed off to Charlie's room. She opened the door and didn't waste any time sinking into his bed. She pulled the sheets over her.

For a few seconds, she thought that she wasn't going to be able to sleep but exhaustion overtook her and soon there was only darkness.

Stacey had been dreaming that she was wading in a pool of water. The ocean was stretched out in front of her. Behind her was Tony's island. She didn't want to go back there. There was an urgency to her wading out deeper in the water, as if Tony's island was trying to pull her back.

She woke suddenly and blinked, trying to clear the fog from her brain. Stacey propped herself up and looked around. The window showed that it was dark outside now. The city twinkled against the darkness.

There was a loud voice followed by low rumbling. That must have been what had woken her up. Stacey threw her legs over the side of the bed and slid out of it, still feeling tired. The carpet felt plush against her feet and kept her footsteps silent as she padded out of the room into the hallway.

"Why aren't you listening to me at all?" It was Eric, sounding more annoyed than she had ever heard him before.

"Because you never say anything important enough to listen to," Charlie snapped in return.

"Will you stop already? Can't even talk to you at all about anything!"

Stacey hesitated. Part of her felt she should go back to bed but she remained glued to the spot. Charlie sounded angry and Eric sounded irritated. Instead of sneaking back into the bedroom, perhaps she should go in and try to break up the fight.

"Listen, that Meredith lady doesn't know what sort of wedding your fiancée wants. How can you want a wedding like that? Some big event?" Eric was saying to her surprise.

"Why don't you mind your own business? I don't remember asking you at all for any advice."

"Well, I'm giving you some because you clearly don't know what you're doing. I could see today that she didn't want a fireworks show or a huge number of guests or whatever else you're adding on."

Charlie's voice was a controlled fury. "If Stacey has an issue with the wedding plans, she can come to me."

"When? You aren't around. Weren't you supposed to meet me here and be part of the wedding planner meeting? But you didn't get home until an hour ago. When would Stacey have told you?"

Charlie said something that Stacey couldn't hear. Eric replied but their voices were distant now as if they were moving to the other side of the penthouse. She felt stuck in place, letting Eric's words wash over her.

It was true, wasn't it? The wedding wasn't what she wanted. It was growing, like a wild beast that couldn't be tamed. But Charlie had a point too – she hadn't told him. As far as he knew, she was only hesitant about the guest list.

Propelling herself forward across the carpet and walking down the long hallway, Stacey heard the voices grow louder. Charlie's office was close by and she could hear them talking in it. The door was halfway shut. Part of her told herself to wait until later to tell Charlie – but she was afraid if she didn't tell him right now that she never would. She would end up going along with this giant wedding she didn't want.

Before she could stop herself, she pushed the door open and stepped into the office. Charlie had his arms crossed and was leaning against the wall behind his desk. Eric was on the opposite side of the room, near one of the bookshelves. Both of them looked at her when she entered.

"Did we wake you up?" Charlie asked, looking abashed.

Stacey cleared her throat, hesitated for just a moment, and then said, "The wedding plans aren't turning out the way I want. It's getting out of hand."

Eric looked victorious, turning to look at Charlie who looked startled by her declaration. He moved toward her and grabbed her arm gently, steering her out of the room. He closed the office door, leaving Eric inside.

"What do you mean?"

"Exactly what I said." The words were rushing out of her mouth now. "It isn't just the guest list. The meeting with Meredith today was overwhelming. All the things she wants – the things Allison wants – the guest list is back up to three hundred because Allison wants to invite Jacob's business partners and investors. It doesn't even feel like our wedding. It feels like a party we're throwing so people can make business connections. Including you," she added gently, remembering how Charlie had said he wanted to invite people who could help his new investment firm.

Charlie looked stunned and his arm dropped from her side. "I had no idea."

"It's okay. I didn't say anything. I should have brought it up again."

"I just assumed. Big weddings… that's what everyone wants, right? I'm sorry," he said. "I didn't mean to upset you."

"I know you meant well. And I thought it would be fun too. But the thought of throwing this massive wedding… Meredith actually had a list of people we should invite and their personality quirks that we should 'tend to'."

Charlie ran his hand over his face. "That's not what I want either. Listen, we'll let it all go. We won't have a wedding like that. We'll do whatever you want. Small wedding. Handful of people. No people at all. We can just go to the courthouse instead."

Stacey looked up at him when he said the last word. He studied her closely.

Then he nodded. "That's right, the courthouse," he said again, this time more confidently.

A buzz of energy swept through her now all the way down to her toes. She couldn't help but smile up at him. "Yes, the courthouse."

Charlie bent down to kiss her when the office door flew open. Eric stood in the doorway. He still had that smug look on his face. Maybe she should have told Charlie when Eric wasn't around, Stacey thought as she looked at his face. Surely Eric was going to use this to drive Charlie even crazier.

But it was too late now.

"You can't just lock me in a room like I'm a kid," Eric scowled. "I'm going to the hotel."

"Good riddance," Charlie sneered.

"You guys, please," Stacey sighed.

Eric wriggled in between the two of them, breaking up their hug as he headed down the hallway. Charlie shook his head and went back into his office, calling Stacey after him. She turned to watch Eric leave. He turned around and began to walk out of the hallway, shooting her a wink before he turned forward and headed into the living room.

Chapter Thirteen

"Are you sure about this?" Charlie asked her for the thousandth time today.

"Yes," Stacey repeated through her smile.

He nodded and exhaled slowly. The car was winding through the city to the courthouse downtown. He was dressed in a suit but kept playing with his tie nervously. Stacey, however, remained calm. She had felt ill earlier in the morning, but it had passed quickly. Now that she was going to marry Charlie, all she could feel were butterflies in her stomach.

It had been five days since they had agreed to forego the large wedding they were planning with Meredith, and had opted for a quiet ceremony at the courthouse instead. Stacey would have been fine going the very next day. But they had to get the wedding license and find rings. Not only that, but Allison was travelling with Jacob out of town for a couple of days and demanded to be there.

"You need a witness," she had proclaimed on the phone, "and I'm the only one who counts."

Stacey had relented. She wanted Allison there. It was the other two hundred and ninety-nine people that she could live without.

Now they were on their way to the courthouse. It was cold outside today with the tree branches stark and a wind slicing its way through the city. Stacey hardly felt it. She was buzzing with excitement.

"Allison is meeting us there, right?" asked Charlie.

"Yeah. She's bringing Jacob as well."

"Great. Are you nervous? I'm nervous," he said.

Stacey smiled. "If you're nervous about this, imagine if we had been married in front of that enormous crowd of people."

"Stupid idea in hindsight." He exhaled slowly through his mouth. "This is better. I can panic in peace."

"I won't tell anyone," Stacey joked, leaning forward and kissing him gently on the cheek.

Charlie turned to look at her. "You look beautiful."

"Thanks. It isn't as extravagant as the dress Meredith would have wanted but I still love it," she replied, gesturing to the simple white dress she was wearing underneath her coat.

Stacey did love it. She had found it downtown while looking for something understated yet pretty. It wasn't technically a wedding dress, but she felt like a bride in it. It had long sleeves made out of lace and beads along the top. In her lap was a small bouquet of red roses that Charlie had given her. She had splurged and gotten her nails done that morning. They were red to match her flowers and reflected the light back at her from the shine of the lacquer.

The car pulled into the parking lot of the courthouse and the driver parked near the front. Charlie got out of the car first and went over to the other side, helping her out of it. The wind cut through her coat and she shivered.

"Winter is definitely coming," Charlie remarked as he pulled his own jacket tighter around him.

"Let's get inside. My toes are going to freeze off." She gestured to her open toed shoes.

He gripped her hand which was warm and a little sweaty. He was really nervous, Stacey thought, as she glanced at him. They walked into the courthouse. Allison was already in the lobby, talking Jacob's ear off. He was standing stiffly next to her, still as pale and dull-looking as ever.

When Allison saw the two of them, she cut her conversation short and rushed over. She crushed Stacey in a hug so hard that she thought her bones were going to pop.

"You look beautiful. Honestly. That dress is really nice."

"Thanks," Stacey said as Jacob went over to Charlie to offer his congrats.

"Come on. I already looked, and we have to go to the second floor. Are you ready?" Allison said, grabbing her wrist and pulling her forward.

Charlie followed at her heels. Jacob had launched into a story about the tea company. Stacey could tell that Charlie was barely listening, just nodding his head a lot. She glanced over at Allison as they piled into the elevator.

She clapped her hands together. "Alright, second floor," she declared so loudly that Jacob stopped speaking as she pressed the button.

The ride was fast, and soon enough they were in a small waiting room. It was empty except for one person.

"What is he doing here?" Stacey asked, wondering if Charlie had invited him.

"No idea," he mumbled before stalking over to where his brother stood.

Eric wasn't dressed up. He was wearing jeans and a baggy yellow t-shirt with some logo Stacey didn't recognize. He had his hands shoved in his pocket. From here she could see the pack of cigarettes in his pocket, straining the fabric. The jeans looked new, Stacey noted, as if he had decided to buy them just for this occasion.

"I should go over there in case Charlie decides to swing," Stacey said to her sister and quickly hurried over.

"–not invited." Charlie was finishing up his lecture.

Eric saw Stacey and smiled brightly at her, as if his brother hadn't just been ranting at him. "You look lovely."

"Thank you."

"You need to go."

"You need a witness."

"We have them." Charlie jerked his head in the direction of Allison and Jacob.

"How did you even find out about this?" Stacey asked curiously.

Eric rolled his eyes. "Meredith. She got my number somehow, can you believe it? She called me up after you let her go. She was spitting mad. Ranting about how she had been disrespected. Anyway, she let it slip that you two were running off to the courthouse sometime this week. After she propositioned me," he had to add.

"Did you say yes?" Stacey wondered at the same time Charlie asked, "How did you find out the time?"

Charlie glanced over at her as if to say *who cares* that Meredith had any interest in Eric. She shrugged and said, "I think it's pretty funny she's so into him."

"Bribes. We have a lot of money, in case you forgot, brother," Eric responded to Charlie first before looking at Stacey. "And no. I had to let her down. Which just made her even angrier."

"Some things just aren't meant to work out," she joked.

Eric laughed at that and even Charlie looked amused before shaking his head and trying to scowl. Stacey rested her hand on his arm to get his attention.

"Just let him stay."

"What?"

"He's your brother. That has to count for something."

"Yeah, come on. I'm your brother," Eric chimed.

Stacey shot him a look that said *shut up, you aren't helping* before turning back to look at Charlie.

"You should have someone of your own at the wedding too. Even if it is Eric."

Charlie paused and then relented, tossing his hands up in the air. "Fine. Fine, he can stay."

"Great," Eric replied, rubbing his hands together.

Someone tapped Stacey on the shoulder. "Sorry to interrupt the family reunion but can I talk to you for a second?"

It was Allison.

"How long until your wedding?" she asked.

Charlie looked at his watch. "Twenty minutes."

"Great, come with me," Allison said, yanking on Stacey's arm toward the hallway.

Confused, Stacey let herself be pulled along. They stopped in front of the bathroom and Allison opened it, pushing Stacey inside. The bathroom wasn't one of those with a lot of stalls but simply a small tiled room with a sink and a toilet. The lighting in it made Stacey look ghastly and she avoided looking in the mirror.

"Okay, what is going on?" Stacey asked, crossing her arms.

Allison was rummaging around in her purse. After a couple of seconds, she pulled something out and handed it to her. Stacey blinked and took it slowly, looking down at it.

"A pregnancy test?"

"You've been sick lately, right?"

It was true. The past few days, Stacey had been feeling ill, even throwing up a couple of times. But she had chalked it up to stress from the wedding. She suddenly felt dizzy.

"Yeah but…"

"Just take it."

"Why now? This could wait."

"You probably waited too long already." She began to feel around Stacey's belly, as if she was far enough along and the baby bump would be easy to feel.

Startled, she smacked Allison's hands away. "Stop! Stop it, you weirdo!"

Allison dropped her hands and laughed. "Whatever. You know it's true. Pee on the stick so you can see if you're pregnant or not. Rather you know now than go into your wedding completely unaware of what's happening with your own body."

"I'm telling you. It's just stress," Stacey said stubbornly as Allison turned to face the corner.

She leaned against the sink, opened the package and read the instructions. She suddenly felt very nervous. Her hands were shaking slightly. She hadn't considered being sick with having anything to do with being pregnant. The instructions seemed to swirl in front of her eyes. She closed them briefly and refocused when she opened them again and looked at her sister.

"I can't pee with you nearby," Stacey snapped.

"Why not?"

"Wait outside. Go stand guard or something."

"Fine, fine." Allison left, closing the bathroom door behind her.

In the sudden silence of the bathroom, Stacey exhaled slowly. Of course her sister couldn't have let this wait. Finding out now or finding out tonight – did it matter? Apparently, this was so urgent that it absolutely had to happen right now, even though Allison had had an entire week to bring this up.

Since Allison had left, it was easier to do the test. Afterward, she knocked twice to let Allison know to come back in. Then she thrust the stick toward her.

"What? I don't want it, fool," Allison said with disgust. "It's covered in your pee. Rest it on the counter."

Stacey obeyed and then asked, "What did you tell the others?"

"Said it was pre-wedding girl stuff." She shrugged. "Charlie is too nervous to care. Eric is too involved in bothering Charlie. And Jacob is just Jacob."

"How is he lately?" she asked, trying to whittle the wait time down with small talk.

"He's okay. He still tends to drone on, but I've been trying to help him see you don't have to yammer on to fill up the silence. It's good to let things breathe."

"Is it weird? Being married to him? Especially when you don't…" She made a small gesture with her hands that really didn't mean anything.

"Love him? I've come to respect him in his own way just like he has with me. I help him with the business sometimes. I think he likes the fact that I'm always honest with him, no matter what. I don't think he gets that with the people who he works with."

"Sounds like everything worked out then."

"Of course it did!" her sister replied flippantly. "I knew it would."

"Right. You always had things figured out."

"Not really. I just had something I was fixated on. Money. Power too, in a way. But this is your day, not mine. Are you nervous?"

"I was before. Now I'm extra nervous," Stacey said, glancing over at the pregnancy test.

"What if it's positive?"

She ran her hand over her belly. "Then I guess I'm having a baby."

Allison smiled. "Tina would be so happy about that. She always wanted you to have kids."

This surprised Stacey. "Really? I didn't know that. She never mentioned anything like that to me."

"Yeah, she would talk about it sometimes. I don't think she ever expected me to have children, so she was hoping you would."

Silence filled the space between the two sisters before Stacey said quietly, "I miss her."

"Me too," Allison replied honestly and then looked at the small watch on her wrist. "Time to check."

Stacey blew air out of her mouth and turned around to the counter. Her sister stood behind her nervously.

She reached out for the test and looked at it. In the tiny screen of the stick, a small plus sign had appeared.

Allison exclaimed something, but Stacey heard a roaring in her ears. She couldn't believe it. She had thought for sure she was just stressed out.

"Hey, hey," her sister's voice was coming back to her now, "are you okay?"

"Just surprised," Stacey said as she stared at the stick.

"Come on. You have to tell Charlie."

"What?" she replied, snapping out of her mood. "We have like ten minutes before our appointment."

"Plenty of time." Allison practically yanked her out of the bathroom.

Stacey was holding the stick in her hand, hardly noticing that she was being tugged back into the waiting room. Pregnant. She was pregnant! It hardly felt real.

Back in the waiting room, Charlie and Eric were listening to Jacob tell a story. Stacey glanced at Allison.

"So much for letting the silence breathe, right?" she joked.

Allison rolled her eyes. "Don't worry about him. Go, go!"

Charlie had seen her by now and was coming over to her. Stacey's heart began to pound in her chest as she stared at him. He looked at her worriedly.

"Are you okay?" He led her away from the rest of the group into the corner of the waiting room. "Are you having second thoughts?"

"No."

"Then what is it?"

His eyes fell on the stick she was clenching in her hand. He frowned in confusion and then attempted to take it away from her. Reflexes kicked in for some reason and Stacey held onto the stick tighter.

Charlie gently pried her fingers open and removed the stick. He raised it up to look at it. Stacey studied him silently. There were two seconds of him letting the information register and then his eyes widened in surprise.

"Is this yours?" he asked, lowering it.

"Well, it's covered in my pee," she blurted out.

"You're pregnant." It came out more as a statement than a question.

She nodded silently and watched him. Was he going to be angry? He hadn't ever brought up children before. But a smile broke out across his face, as radiant as the sun. Charlie leaned over and brought her in for a hug. He held her tightly before suddenly letting her go.

"Sorry. Sorry. The baby. I shouldn't be…" He trailed off and smiled at her again. "We're going to be parents."

"Well, I'll go to the doctor. To confirm it," she said quickly.

"I believe it's right." He smiled at her.

Allison came over then. "Sorry to interrupt but we have to get going. They called your name already."

Charlie looked back at Stacey. She was so nervous that she thought she might faint. Her brain was battling so many different emotions that her head felt light. Charlie grabbed hold of her hand tightly, as if he was never going to let go.

Together, they headed toward the room to be married.

Chapter Fourteen

The next week, Allison hosted a small get together at Jacob's place. It was mostly a business dinner, but Stacey was looking forward to going anyway. She liked seeing her sister. On top of that, she had been so busy since she had gotten married that she hardly had any time to enjoy herself.

After moving in with Charlie, Stacey had put her apartment up for sale. It felt odd saying good-bye to the place. She had cried on the floor of what had been Tina's room and had trailed through the apartment like a ghost. There had been a lot of memories, both good and bad.

On top of moving, she had been helping William at work. Stacey had found herself hitting a groove there that made the long days go by quickly. She was working quickly, keeping herself organized and task-oriented. It felt different from the other jobs she had, even the short time she worked for Tony.

After going to the doctor and confirming her pregnancy, Stacey knew there was even more that would have to get done. They would have to redecorate one of the rooms for the baby, for one thing. Stacey had to deal with being sick in the mornings, and she worried about feeling even worse as more time went on.

Even so, she was in a fantastic mood when they arrived at the small party. Her sister was glowing in a light blue dress lined with lace. Jacob was by her side as always. To her relief, there were no signs of Tony or Adele. She hadn't seen them since the last party here, when Charlie had proposed.

Eric had wangled his way into the event. Stacey assumed that it was because her sister seemed to have a soft spot for him, although who knew why. Her sister loved troublemakers and general annoyances; both which described Eric.

Charlie had been busy trying to train Eric on the business, but had told her he wasn't having much luck.

"It's like he doesn't care at all," Charlie had said to her the other night. "I mean, he's made it perfectly clear he wanted this over the years. Now he has it and he's acting like it's ruining his day."

"I don't get it," Stacey had replied. "Doesn't make much sense. Are you worried?"

"When it comes to Eric, I'm always worried," he said with a resigned tone.

Now, however, he offered a small wave to his brother from across the room. Eric waved back but was clearly busy trying to charm a tall, pretty woman.

"Is that all your brother does?" she asked Charlie.

"Flirt? Yeah, basically. Never understood how it comes so easily to him. I always tried to be careful.

People hear you have money and that's all they care about."

Stacey watched Eric laugh and lean in toward to the woman. He had a slight smile on his face and was holding a glass of whiskey in one hand. *Because he doesn't care if they just want his money,* she thought to Charlie, *he doesn't care about much at all.*

"Great! You're here!" Allison had seen them and swooped over, hugging Charlie and kissing Stacey on her cheek. "I put some sparkling grape soda aside for you," she said in a low voice. "That way you look like you're drinking and no one will notice you aren't. Better to keep the pregnancy a secret as long as you can."

"You sure know your stuff," Charlie replied.

"Are you telling me that I'm wrong?" Allison asked, almost defensively.

He shook his head. "No, not at all. You're right. We don't want everyone to know yet."

"Great, you go mingle," she ordered Charlie. "I want some time with my sister."

She pulled Stacey toward the kitchen. Stacey waved at Charlie and allowed herself to be pulled inside. The massive kitchen was brimming with servers and people preparing food. They greeted Allison when she came in.

"Why are you always pulling me around like a dog?" Stacey joked, loosening her arm from Allison's grip.

"You overthink things and move too slowly," she replied as she opened the fridge.

"Good point."

Allison pulled out the soda and poured her some in a champagne flute and handed it to her. Stacey thanked her and took a sip.

"Do you remember…" Allison started to say.

"Drinking this stuff as kids and pretending it was wine?" Stacey finished.

Allison laughed, "We drank so much our mouths were purple. We looked so silly."

Stacey grinned, replying, "We had purple tongues for hours. Tina was so annoyed."

Allison looped her arm through Stacey's. "Come on. Let's head out."

<<◇>>

Halfway through the party, Stacey was actually feeling a little queasy. It didn't help that, like always, more people had shown up, making the penthouse feel crowded. She brushed it aside. The last thing she wanted was to leave early.

She looked over at Charlie and Eric, who were currently laughing at the fact they had stuck a sticker on Jacob's back and he hadn't noticed. Both were drunk. It was such a rare sight to see them both getting along that there was no way Stacey was going to cut that short.

Charlie was laughing so hard that he snorted which only made Eric laugh harder. She couldn't hear what they were saying, but they kept gesturing to Jacob. The sticker they had stuck to his back was of a baby wearing a silly party hat, exclaiming 'Happy New Year!' Stacey had no idea where in the world they had found something like that.

Jacob had no idea the sticker was on his back. The longer it went on, the more the two brothers laughed. Stacey tried to find the resemblance between them. Their eyes crinkled the same way when they were laughing, she decided. But that was about it.

Allison came out of the side hallway and saw what they were laughing about. Her face flushed and she stormed over to Jacob. Then she casually circled her arm around his waist and swiftly pulled the sticker off. Jacob didn't notice anything at all.

Bunching up the sticker, she moved away from Jacob and went over to the two brothers. Stacey watched as she flicked the sticker at Eric and began to lecture the two of them. They were too drunk to care however, and Allison gave up.

That was when she saw Stacey sitting in the corner. She went over to her and sat in the chair next to her.

"I saw," Stacey said before her sister tried to explain.

"What is up with them?"

"They're drunk."

"And getting along. And making a fool out of Jacob."

Stacey took a sip from her glass. Peering over the rim, she widened her eyes innocently to hide the fact that she found it amusing.

Allison shrugged, "At least they're getting along, right?"

"Do you think it'll stick?" Stacey asked curiously.

"No, probably not. Everything is better when you're drunk. But reality will kick in eventually."

"Yeah," Stacey replied, feeling disappointed. "True, I guess."

She looked back over at the brothers. Her stomach tightened hard suddenly, and she winced and rubbed her belly.

"You okay?" Allison asked.

"Crowded in here."

"Tell me about it. We're going to run out of food," she grumbled.

Stacey forced a smile through her discomfort but managed to say, "I'm okay. Go, tend to the guests."

"Alright. If you need me though, find me."

"Will do."

Stacey watched her sister head back into the fray. She turned to look over at Charlie, but the brothers were gone. She stood up to try to find them and make sure they weren't getting into more trouble. When she stood up, however, a wave of dizziness swept over. Stacey closed her eyes. It was hot in here, she realized.

Charlie and Eric were big boys. They could handle themselves. In the meantime, she needed some fresh air. She walked out to the balcony. There was a cluster of people on one side of it, smoking cigars. Stacey opted to go to the opposite side where it was more secluded.

She pulled a chair close to the edge of railing of the balcony and sat down. Allison had a great view. Even now, married to Charlie and pregnant with his child, there were some things about her new life that still took her by surprise. Small things, like a view such as this, was one of them.

It was chilly outside with winter quickly approaching. But Stacey's skin felt hot and the cold against her skin was pleasant. Her stomach was grumbling, as if she hadn't eaten just an hour ago. The last thing she wanted was to be sick here tonight. Not with Charlie having a good time.

There was a loud boom of laughter and Stacey looked over at the group of people on the other side of the balcony. Eric was in the middle of them now, a cigar hanging out of his lips as he told them a story. She couldn't hear it, but it must have been hilarious. She wondered where Charlie was.

Eric finished the story and was listening to someone else speaking when he saw Stacey. He took the cigar out of his mouth and handed it to a woman next to him. Then he walked over to her.

"Where's Charlie?" she asked him.

"He's inside. He drank way too much and thought he was going to be sick," Eric grinned.

"And you?"

"I'm drunk but I never get sick."

"Is that so?" Stacey asked dryly.

Eric pulled a chair up next to hers and sat down. He was fiddling with his lighter, most likely resisting the urge to smoke around her.

"What are you doing out here?"

"I didn't feel too well inside. It was a bit too crowded."

"You should tell Charlie so you two can leave before you both start getting sick at the same time," he remarked, looking over the balcony.

"Yeah, I will," she said, trying to ignore the sick feeling that was blooming in her stomach.

"So," he said, leaning back in his chair. "You excited? For the kid, I mean. I heard that's exciting, anyway."

"Yeah, I'm really excited," Stacey replied honestly. "I still can't believe it."

"Lots of changes coming," Eric said and something in his voice made her look at him more closely.

"Yeah. All good changes though. Even for you. I mean, you're finally getting to control the company, right?"

Eric let out a dry laugh, "Yeah, sure."

She frowned, "What does that mean?"

He cleared his throat and then leaned toward her. She could smell the booze wafting off of him. When he spoke, she could smell it off of his mouth.

"It means that this is all bullshit."

"What is?"

"All of it. Didn't I tell you before? Dad isn't just going to let Charlie walk away. He'll interfere with Charlie soon enough. Then he will have to come back to the company. He'll become president again."

"Why? I don't get it. Why doesn't your dad just let it go?"

"No one goes against our father, Stace. No one. Not even his sons."

"That's why you aren't taking anything seriously," she said, realization dawning on her.

He snapped his fingers. "Bingo," he slurred.

Stacey shook her head. "Charlie needs to know this."

She went to get up when Eric's hand grabbed her arm. The touch was sudden, and she stopped, looking down at him.

"Didn't you warn him?"

"What?"

"I told you this before. About Dad not letting this slide." His voice was a little more urgent now. "You told him, didn't you?"

"What? No." She sat back down next to Eric because he looked as if he was turning an ugly shade of green. "I just thought he would know."

"I told you so you would tell him!"

"You tell him!" she snapped. "How was I supposed to know you meant for me to tell him?"

"Why didn't you tell him?" Eric asked, his head lolling drunkenly to one side before turning to look at her.

Stacey hesitated and then replied, "He doesn't like us getting along, I think. It bothers him. I thought if he knew we talked about it, he'd be angry."

Eric stared at her but didn't saying anything. He looked as if he wanted to say something, but no words came out. Stacey stared back at him for a few seconds before standing up.

"I have to get Charlie," she said, fighting another wave of dizziness.

Eric stood up now. "I'll come with you."

They walked back into the apartment. The crowd had thinned a little. Allison was talking to someone near the kitchen. Jacob was sitting at a table with an old man. They were looking at what appeared to be a map. Stacey didn't even want to know what that was about.

They headed down one of the hallways. Stacey thought of how she had been down this hallway before. She had been looking for Charlie then too. Tony had been trailing after her and had cornered her in the library. She pushed the thought from her mind.

They stopped at one of the bathrooms and knocked. There was no answer.

"Charlie? It's Stacey."

This time there was a groaning noise and the door unlocked. She pushed herself in and found Charlie slouched over the toilet, looking worse for wear. Behind her, she could hear Eric snickering.

"Come on," she said, knowing she wasn't going to be able to discuss Terry with him in this state. "We're going home."

"Good idea. I think I drank too much," Charlie mumbled.

"Never could hold the booze," Eric boasted.

"Just shut up and help me," she said to him.

The two of them went over to Charlie and helped him to his feet. He leaned back against the wall and steadied himself on Stacey.

"Never seen you this drunk before."

"Eric brings the worst out in me," Charlie hiccupped.

"Are you going to tell him?" Eric nudged her.

She tried not to feel irritated and glared at him. She knew he was just as drunk but hopefully, Eric would get the point and shut up.

"Tell me what?"

"Nothing," Stacey replied.

But Eric was too drunk to let it go. He pushed past her and got in Charlie's face. "Dad is gonna fuck up your business."

"Huh?"

"Eric, not now," she snapped.

"No – yes, I mean. Yes, now. Dad isn't serious about me learning about the business from you. Or learning about it period. He said it's pointless," he slurred. "He's going to take away anyone interested in your company until you come crawling back to be president."

"What?" Charlie mumbled, his eyes widening drunkenly at the two of them.

Eric kept going on, much to Stacey's chagrin. "I shouldn't even be telling you this. I told Stacey and I thought – I thought she'd tell you, dude. You gotta come back or you'll just get run into the ground. Dad harps on you all the time but he doesn't want me in charge of the company!"

Charlie was looking at her now. "You knew about this?" he asked, sounding as if he was sobering up magically.

"He told me that your father was going to do something like this, yes, although I had no idea Eric wasn't taking it seriously for those reasons."

He nudged past Eric and came close to her. He stunk of alcohol and vomit, and his eyes were glazed over. That cold sick feeling was spreading across her body. Her back pressed up against the counter and she gripped it with her hands behind her.

"Why didn't you tell me?"

"I thought you knew."

Stacey felt as if someone had splashed cold water on her insides.

"Charlie, wait," she said, trying to explain. "I thought you knew going into it that your dad would be like this."

She couldn't bring herself to tell him just yet that she hadn't told him because he had already seemed to be jealous of Eric being friendly with her. The fact he had warned her had just seemed like it would upset Charlie. She had been trying to do the right thing. But he looked away from her.

Charlie shook his head and without another word he stumbled from the bathroom. She watched him go, feeling upset.

She spun on Eric who was slouching in the corner. "Why did you tell him?"

"I thought that's why we were going to find him," he said with eyes wide open.

"He's drunk! He didn't have to hear that now. I have to go get him," she mumbled mostly to herself and turned around.

"Stacey, wait," Eric said, clamoring after her before she could leave, "I have to tell you something. Don't go just yet."

She whirled on him, angrier than she should be and lashing out at Eric, "Let me tell you something. I am not a messenger. If you have to tell your brother something, then tell him yourself instead of going through me. I tried to do the right thing. I just didn't want to upset him. And now he's probably furious with me all because you didn't have the balls to do your own dirty work!"

Eric had the good sense to look abashed even though he was hiccupping now. "I'm sorry."

"I have to go get him. So whatever you have to tell me, tell me quickly." Her words were harsh even to her own ears.

"Stacey, listen, I…"

But she didn't hear whatever Eric ended up saying because suddenly her stomach kicked up in such pain that she doubled over, clutching her mid-riff. It felt as if her entire body was going to collapse into itself. She sunk to her knees.

Eric was panicked now, hovering over her and opening the bathroom door, calling for help. He sounded far away. Stacey was hunched over with her nose practically touching the floor. The pain was so intense that she was worried she was going to black out.

People were coming to the door now. She wasn't sure who was behind her. The only thing she could focus on was the acute pain in her body. Something else was nagging her at the back of her mind – a sensation that was sticking out from above the rest.

Her sister's voice swam to the front of her brain and Stacey managed to raise her face enough to look at her. Allison was asking her questions, but Stacey couldn't reply. Then Allison's eyes cast down and she made a horrified strangled noise.

Stacey looked down to see what had scared her sister. At first, she just saw something dark on the floor – a few spots, nothing more.

But then it clicked through the pain.

It was blood, dripping out of the bottom of her dress.

-To be continued in Book 5-

If you enjoyed this title, I would appreciate your leaving a review of the book. Good reviews encourage an author to write as well as help books to sell. Good reviews can be just a few short sentences describing what you liked about the book without having a spoiler. If you could spend 30 seconds writing a review, I would appreciate it: you can review this title right now at your favorite retailer.

Here is a preview of the **next book** you may also enjoy:

"**WALK SLOWLY**. Maybe you should wait here. I can get a wheelchair."

"From where?" Stacey asked. "I'm fine, really."

Charlie frowned and reached out for her anyway. He slid his arm around her waist to help her walk into the lobby of their apartment complex. Stacey knew that she could walk fine without his help but didn't want to shrug him off.

She had spent the night in the hospital. There were those terrifying moments that Stacey had been utterly convinced something dreadful had happened to the baby. She felt sore all over as if a train hit her.

But the doctor said the baby was okay. She was a high-risk pregnancy and would have to take things slowly. He told her to cut back on work and stress. Stacey couldn't help but think of Charlie and his family, her new job with William, and Charlie's own investment firm starting up. Cut back on stress. How in the world was she going to do that?

There was no time to talk to Charlie about what his brother, Eric, had told her. Eric warned her that their father, Terry, was going to move against Charlie. At the time, Stacey decided not to tell Charlie because she didn't want to upset him. Now that Eric had drunkenly blathered about it, she saw it in a new light. Charlie perceived it as Stacey keeping a secret from him, something she only shared with Eric, his brother, of all people.

As they made their way up to the penthouse, she wondered how she should apologize and try to make what happened clear to him. Charlie, who became incredibly drunk last night, was now extremely hungover. His skin was sick looking, with a slight yellow tinge to it. His hair was messy and he still wore the same clothes from the other night. He was now drinking water and coffee non-stop. Both of them needed a nap.

At home, Charlie led her directly to bed. Stacey sunk into the massive bed gratefully, pulling the sheets over her. She knew that she needed to talk to him about Eric and what he had said, but she suddenly felt more exhausted than ever. Everything that had happened seemed to sweep over her all at once and she felt as if she had emotional whiplash.

"Charlie…" she mumbled as he crawled into bed next to her.

"It's okay," he whispered back and brought her close against him.

Stacey could hear the steady beat of his heart. Her eyelids closed without effort. All her limbs felt as if they each weighed a thousand pounds. Before she could utter another word, she fell fast asleep.

<<◇>>

In her dream, there was a baby crying in the distance. Stacey knew that this was hers. She was in Tina's old house, at the dining room table. She felt rooted to the chair as if she couldn't move. Next to her was Allison. She was ignoring her homework again, covering her page in doodles.

Stacey could hear the TV playing in the living room. Some part of her realized this was the night she found out about her parents' deaths. The baby cried louder in the distance.

Fighting against the pull that was keeping her to her chair, she managed to stand up. Allison didn't glance at her – it was as if Stacey wasn't even there. Stacey felt hot all over, as though she suddenly came down with a fever.

The phone rang. She knew what the news was going to be. Quickly, she darted out of the dining room. If she kept running, she wouldn't have to hear the news. She just had to keep moving.

She ran to the front door and yanked it open. Behind her, Tina was letting out a wailing cry. Stacey stepped outside and slammed the door shut. The front yard was covered in a thick layer of snow. The moon was covered by clouds and almost everything was dark.

She cut across the yard. The crying got louder now. She could see a cradle in the distance. She hurried, anxious to get to it.

But as Stacey approached the cradle, a sharp pain shot through her body. It felt like she was getting stabbed. Her knees weakened and she hit the ground. The snow around her turned red. She let out a gasp.

"You're okay! You're okay, Stacey. It was just a dream."

Stacey's eyes opened and she found herself staring up at Charlie. His arms were wrapped firmly around her, and he was clutching her close to his chest. Her breathing was coming hard and fast as if she just ran a mile. She could still see the snow around her, turning dark with her own blood as her baby in the cradle cried.

She shivered and said, "I'm okay. Sorry. Did I wake you up?"

"Yeah. You were making a whimpering noise." He pushed back a strand of hair that fell in front of her eyes. "You sounded terrified."

Stacey's mouth felt dry, as if it was stuffed full of cotton. The room was dark except for the hallway light shining through the crack in the door. They must have forgotten to shut it off when they got home.

"What time is it?" she asked.

"Little after three in the morning."

"And I woke you up. I'm sorry," she said again.

"Hey, it's okay. Really. Do you want to talk about the dream?"

Stacey thought about Tina answering that phone call that changed everything. The thought of her parents and Tina, now all gone, made her heart ache. She silently shook her head. Charlie nodded and then got out of bed.

"Need some water. Want some?"

"Yes, please."

She watched him go and tried to calm down her racing heart. She told herself it was just a dream. She had weird dreams all the time. This one was no different. How could she not have crazy dreams after what she just went through?

Stacey sat up and brought the blanket around her. It was slightly chilly in the room. She reached over to check her phone. There were two missed calls from Allison, who left shortly before Stacey was discharged from the hospital. She left only because Jacob's father recently fell and had been sent to a hospital out of state. Stacey ordered her sister to leave, telling her over and over again that she was fine and so was the baby. Stacey felt it was important for Allison to be with Jacob.

She made a mental note to call Allison first thing to try to calm her nerves. She could picture her sister right now, nervously pacing the hotel room, torn between her and Jacob.

Charlie came back with two glasses of water and handed one to her. Then he sat down next to her and took a swig from his glass. Stacey mumbled a thank you and drank half of her water in one gulp. She was incredibly thirsty for some reason.

"I shouldn't have stormed out of the party like that," he finally said.

Out of everything for him to say, Stacey was surprised by this. She wasn't even thinking about how he hadn't been there right at the start of things. She was too busy trying to form an apology in her head.

"You don't have to be sorry," she replied.

"Yeah, I do. If I'd stayed – if I'd stayed even a minute longer…" he trailed off.

Stacey grabbed his hand, shaking her head. "No, Charlie. It wouldn't have changed anything."

"If I hadn't gotten angry with you over what Eric said. Being drunk isn't an excuse. I should have stopped myself and discussed it with you. Instead, I got angry and you ended up in the hospital."

"One has nothing to do with the other," she said firmly.

But Charlie shrugged and looked morosely at his glass before saying, "Maybe not."

"They don't. And even if you were there, nothing would have changed. Eric found you a minute later, didn't he?"

"I know. I know it's pointless to beat myself up over it. I was terrified that you were hurt or something happened to the baby."

"Well, I'm okay. I just need to relax."

"You're so good at that," he joked and smiled at her.

"Well, just keep me in check." She poked his abs playfully and smiled back.

Charlie leaned over and kissed her gently before saying, "I'm sorry that I got angry. I'm basically sorry for the entire night. Made me remember why I don't drink like that."

"No, I'm sorry for not telling you about what Eric warned me about."

She hesitated for a moment and then decided to tell him the entire thing. She told him of how Eric had warned her about Terry not being pleased back in the hallway at the manor. She admitted to slapping him and feeling ashamed at having done so. Stacey then finished with Eric telling her that his becoming president was bullshit and wouldn't happen.

Charlie leaned back in bed. "I knew there must have been a reason why Eric wasn't taking things seriously. I mean, don't get me wrong. He never takes things seriously. But this was different. This was something he had been saying for years he deserved. It lands in his lap yet he doesn't want it? It didn't make sense."

"What are you going to do about your father?"

He shrugged. "Ignore him."

"No, Charlie, I'm serious."

"So am I."

Stacey shook her head. "Eric seems to be taking this really seriously. When he mentioned it in the hallway, I just assumed he was trying to start things and that you knew already what Terry was up to. But you don't. You could lose this entire business before it even gets off the ground."

If you enjoyed this sample then look for **Love Divine: Persuasive Billionaire BWWM Romance Series, Book 5**.

Here is a preview of **another story** you may enjoy:

"**WHAT DID** you say?" Adalia adjusted her son, her gorgeous little Isaac, on her breast and stared at Dr. Matheson as if he'd grown an extra head.

Trent's hand gripped her shoulder, fingernails digging into the flesh. She glanced up at him but he didn't meet her gaze… he was slack-jawed, cheeks pale.

Dr. Matheson heaved a sigh and Adalia shifted her focus back to him, holding Isaac close, appreciating the smell of his tan skin and the gentle suckling noises he made as he fed.

"I'm afraid that your son is ill." Matheson cleared his throat. "Please, Mr. Dawson, take a seat."

Trent seemed resistant to the idea – his grip on her shoulder trembled for a few seconds – but he sank to the chair beside her bed, slipping his hand down to rest on her forearm.

"He's ill…" Adalia repeated, stroking a finger over Isaac's forehead. "He can't be ill. He's perfect."

"This is going to be difficult for you to hear, Mrs. Dawson. Perhaps one of the nurses can take Isaac for a rest while we discuss it."

A nurse bustled through the doors at the end of the ward on cue, smiling with a pity smile. Trent went rigid beside her bed and shuddered again. "You will not touch my son," he growled at her.

"Trent," Adalia whispered. "Relax. Let's hear what the doctor has to say." She had to remain calm for her son's sake. She wouldn't risk upsetting him, even though her insides were knotted with anxiety.

Dr. Matheson worked his jaw, trying to articulate but failing. The nurse stayed by the door, gaze darkening thanks to Trent's snappy comment. She folded her arms and looked to Matheson for guidance, as if he could override the father's wishes. *Stupid bitch.*

"Spit it out," Trent said.

Matheson jerked and readjusted his white coat. "Isaac has an abnormally high white blood cell count. Conversely, his red blood cell count is low. We need to perform a biopsy to ascertain exactly what these results mean."

"What are the possibilities?" Adalia asked, arms pulling her son closer still. He suckled and smacked his lips, then popped off her breast, falling fast asleep. She covered her chest absentmindedly.

"Cancer. Leukemia specifically." Matheson showed them his palms at the exact moment Trent leapt to his feet. "But we need to do the tests first."

"What else could it be? What else?"

"An autoimmune deficiency, but that's highly unlikely. He doesn't have any rashes and hasn't had seizures." Matheson flipped the file open to study the paperwork again, but it was obviously his method of avoiding their shocked gazes.

Panic gathered in the center of Adalia's chest, a leaden ball which threatened to drop through her and drag tears down her cheeks. She welled up and used one hand to dab beneath her eyes. She didn't want to cry with Matheson and the nurse in the room.

"So you're telling us it can only be leukemia."

"It's the most likely outcome," Matheson conceded. "I'm sure you understand this is a serious prognosis and should it be confirmed, we'll have to deal with it accordingly."

"What are our options?" Adalia asked, swallowing to stop the tears. She swallowed and swallowed but the lump in her throat wouldn't go away. She looked at Trent. His face was lined with anger, his go-to reaction when he couldn't deal.

"I'd much rather discuss that after we have confirmed the prognosis."

"You'll tell us now," Trent commanded. "You will tell us right now, Dr. Matheson, otherwise you will kindly explain why you brought this up prior to ascertaining whether Isaac has leukemia or not."

"Calm down," Adalia murmured. Tears spilled from her eyes. "Just calm down."

Matheson stared at them, opening and closing his mouth again. "There's a new therapy which could successfully cure Isaac should he have leukemia."

"What is it?" Adalia asked immediately, trying but failing to rid herself of the tears. "We'll do anything."

"We managed to preserve some of Isaac's stem cells, found in the umbilical cord. Simply put, the treatment involves an injection of these stem cells into Isaac's bone marrow."

"Then let's do that. We'll do that," Trent said, settling back as if the matter was dealt with. Her husband was all bravado and self-belief, but the fear coursed behind his façade. If it wasn't anger protecting him, it was the business-like confidence.

Little Isaac mewled once and went back to sleep, sucking on thin air with his curved lips parted. Her precious baby. She couldn't let anything happen to him. She would rather die. She would trade her life for his in a heartbeat.

"It's an exceptionally expensive treatment on the frontier of cancer research, Mr. Dawson." Matheson delivered the blow in a lowered voice, a croaking whisper which the sullen nurse wouldn't be able to overhear.

"And so? I'm a billionaire. I think we'll be okay." Trent tried to reassure the others but his shoulders had dropped. Space Inc. had taken a hit because of the shuttle explosion, hopefully not too big of a hit. Trent had invested more than just his time in getting that craft into the air.

"Do I have your permission to proceed with the test?"

"Will it be painful for him?" Adalia clutched the baby to her chest again, shifting him so that he was vertical with his head resting below her collar bone.

"There will be a certain level of pain involved."

The nurse stepped forward from her spot beside the door and Adalia gripped Isaac tighter. She gave the woman a warning look, gritting her teeth.

"Please, Mrs. Dawson, this is the only way to know for sure." Matheson gave her a warm smile, encouraging, but it didn't make a damn difference to her. She didn't want to give her baby up to anyone, least of all the nurse with the eager stare.

"Adalia," Trent said, rising beside her. "Give Isaac to me." He took the baby from her carefully, holding him like precious cargo, and walked over to the nurse.

The nurse took Isaac and he woke in her arms. He kicked his little legs, waved his fists in the air, struggling to be free of his receiving blanket. Isaac cried, two sharp wails which turned into a full-blown bawl.

"Give him back," Adalia said, the tears coming again, racking her body. She sobbed, watching helplessly as the nurse took her screaming son and walked out of the room. "I need him close to me. Bring back my baby!"

Trent rushed to her side and wrapped his arms around, resting his head on her shoulder. "It's okay, honey, it's going to be okay. We'll make him better."

"I'll leave you two alone," Dr. Matheson said. "I'm so sorry, Mr. and Mrs. Dawson." He tipped his head and walked for the door with short steps.

Trent rocked Adalia backwards and forwards, soothing her with subtle coos and words. "We have the money to make this happen. Isaac is going to be okay."

How could he possibly know that?

Adalia couldn't speak. She couldn't think. All she could process were Isaac's distant cries which rang in her ears, driving her deeper and deeper into despair.

If you enjoyed this sample then look for **Love Everlasting: Tenacious Billionaire BWWM Romance Series, Book 4**.

Here is a preview of **another story** you may enjoy:

Love Restrained: Fervent Billionaire BWWM Romance Series, Book 1

"EXHALE SLOWLY," the yoga instructor said in a soothing voice. Alexandra exhaled her breath and relaxed her muscles. As she exhaled, she consciously focused on releasing all of her worries. Her body was in the bridge pose, so her navel faced the twirling ceiling fan.

"Inhale through your nose," came the second instruction. Alexandra inhaled and the sound of her breath filled her ears. She held the pose for what seemed like a lifetime as the base of her neck pressed against the floor.

"Release," came the blessed instruction, finally. Automatically, Alexandra moved into corpse pose. She had been practicing yoga for three months and was finally feeling confident about her poses. She knew that there was still a long way to go, but she was getting there. Her mind was relaxed as she felt the warm caress of the sunlight travel along her torso. A smile spread across her face as she focused on existing entirely in the moment. Without thought, she moved fluidly between all of the yoga positions.

Her eyes opened and her mind returned when the instructor ended the session, "Thank you for attending, *Namaste.*"

"*Namaste,*" Alexandra replied with her palms together. As she rolled up her mat, she looked around at the other patrons. All were covered in sweat, all wearing modern yoga shorts and tops. Only the instructor wore the loose-fitting, traditional clothes of *Kundalini* yoga. Karen, the instructor, stood at the head of the class in conversation with a few of the patrons.

Turning away from everyone else, Alexandra studied her figure in the large mirror that lined the wall of the room. Her eyes wandered across her own body and she felt pleasure at seeing the results of her many yoga sessions. The pink and black yoga pants fit perfectly along her dark calves and hips. Slender, yet toned, she admired her own hourglass figure in the mirror. Her eyes glanced at her glistening ebony skin and the few beads of sweat that dotted her skin from the overly warm room. She released her curly hair from the clasp of a bun and watched as it cascaded down her shoulders.

With a broad smile, she turned to leave the room. She walked toward the door and placed her hand on the warm metal doorknob. As the door pushed forward, she looked over her shoulder to say goodbye to her instructor. She noticed Karen and a man speaking with each other, their eyes looking at Alexa's toned figure. Dismissing the glances, she turned away with a cheery wave.

A few blocks down the street was her favorite café, the one that she went to after yoga class. As she walked there, she could feel the eyes of other people watching her—mostly men. Not long ago after making a steady income, she had moved to a more upscale segment of town. As one of the few African-Americans in town, she drew stares that ranged from curious to desirous whenever she went out. She did not mind the ogling, but it was the catcalls that ate at her. Catcalls were so vulgar and seemed cowardly. If someone wanted to speak to her, then she would prefer that they were up front with her. She felt that a real man would be one who says what he means and does not just yell something out of a speeding car window.

If you enjoyed this sample then look for **Love Restrained: Fervent Billionaire BWWM Romance Series, Book 1**.

Other Books by Shyla Starr

- Tenacious Billionaire BWWM Romance Series

- Elusive Billionaire Romance Series

- Lonely Billionaire Romance Series

- Ardent Billionaire Romance Series

- Fervent Billionaire BWWM Romance Series

- Audacious Billionaire BWWM Romance Series

Get the latest update on new releases from the author at:

https://shylastarr.com/newsletter/

About the Author - Shyla Starr

Shyla currently specializes in writing interracial romance stories and is a huge fan of the alpha male. Simply put, there just aren't enough stories about mixed couple romances, which is something she is aiming to fix.

Being a bookworm all her life, when Shyla discovered men she also realized how easy it was to fulfill her fantasies through her writing.

When not writing and fantasizing about men, Shyla enjoys dancing, reading and chilling with her friends.

Connect with Shyla Starr

I really appreciate you reading my book! Here are my social media coordinates:

Friend me on Facebook:
https://www.facebook.com/shylastarrauthor

Follow me on Twitter: https://twitter.com/shylstarr

Check me out on Goodreads:
https://www.goodreads.com/author/show/8436084.Shyla_Starr

Subscribe to my newsletter:
https://shylastarr.com/newsletter/

Visit my website: https://shylastarr.com/

www.ingramcontent.com/pod-product-compliance
Lightning Source LLC
Chambersburg PA
CBHW021158110726
47900CB00002B/631